To Eveline,

Hope you enjoy! ...

Carol

D.N.A.

By

Neroli

iUniverse
New York   Bloomington

D.N.A

iUniverse books may be ordered through booksellers or by contacting:

iUniverse
1663 Liberty Drive
Bloomington, IN 47403
www.iuniverse.com
1-800-Authors (1-800-288-4677)

This is a work of fiction. All of the characters, names, incidents, organizations, and dialogue in this novel are either the products of the author's imagination or are used fictitiously.

ISBN: 978-0-595-51678-0(pbk)
ISBN: 978-0-595-50642-2(cloth)
ISBN: 978-0-595-61990-0 (ebk)

Printed in the United States of America

Shoot for the moon even if you miss
you'll land among the stars.

- Les Brown -

PROLOGUE

My mother's steel hand was aiming for my face again. A scene I had experienced way too often. Instantaneously, I decided it would no longer happen. This was it. A fraction of a second before that steel hand could have contact with my face. I ran towards the door screaming; "NO! No more! I can't take this anymore!"

I rushed out the door and ran as fast as I could without looking back. I knew the woods well. I had lived in this part of the Echo Bay forest for over seven years.

The forest consisted mainly of evergreens. A carpet of copper colour pine needles covered the ground, keeping it puddle free and also silencing my steps as I ran through the trees. The air was crisp this late in the evening; it always got cooler when the sun went down. I knew the quickest way out and long ago had planned a hiding spot for this very moment. This time of the year, the ground was mostly dry, making my journey less slippery, as I followed a trail I knew like the back of my hand. Although the light was disappearing as the sun was setting, I still knew when to jump to avoid stumbling on rocks or tree limbs and when to bend my head low, dodging branches that whipped by me as I ran through the trees. A few kilometres later I entered my secret cave, where I had planned to hide until morning.

I didn't want the cops or anyone else to find me. They would just bring me back and that was the last thing I wanted. Everything was ready for this final night. I had reviewed this plan in my head a million times. A few years after we moved to this place, I found this cave approximately a half hour run from my parents' shack. When I first came up with my plan, I started hiding items I knew would come in handy for my escape and slowly built my getaway kit; a change of clothes, scissors, eyeglasses, make-up, baseball cap. Everything was in

Ziploc bags to keep them dry and bug free. Every morning, I routinely strapped to my body all my belongings with which I did not want to part. It was so little and so easily concealed under all the layers of clothes I wore daily. No one could ever have suspected I was planning to run away. I did not know when it would happen, until that very moment. I simply could not endure one more second of my parents' abuse.

We lived in a log house built by my father when we first moved there seven years earlier. After my father got fired from his millionth job, he decided to get away from it all. He could no longer get a job anywhere because everyone knew he had a drinking problem. So he decided to give everything up and drag my mother and me deep into the woods where no one would find us. This old weathered log house was located in the middle of the forest, I mean literally in the middle of nowhere. You might think that a seven-year-old house is not that old but wood when unprotected quickly dries out and turns grey.

Very few people knew we lived there, if any. The first three months we lived in tents while my father cut down trees to build the house. You can imagine the cold drafts coming through in the winter. The only heat we had was from a homemade fireplace in one corner of the cabin. The only dividing walls in the place separated my parents' bedroom from the rest of the house. We lived as hermits, no electricity, and no running water. I didn't even have a room. I slept on the couch or in a corner until they finally went to their own room. We got water from a spring source in the forest, and when that was frozen we melted snow and ice in a pot on the stove. There was an outhouse about thirty feet away from the main house where I also bathed when I wasn't able to slip a quick shower at the motel where I worked. The outhouse was the only place I could get any privacy. Life was really rough but somehow I knew there was something better out there and I was determined to acquire it for myself. If my parents preferred to live like pigs that was their business but I sure wasn't going to keep living like this longer than I had to.

Both my parents were unemployed and drank every moment they were awake. The only family income was from firewood my father had me chop during the summer months. He would cut down the trees, usually late afternoon or early evening while there was still some light out, and then I would cut it into firewood. He had started teaching me the first summer we moved here and as I got stronger and more capable he slowly stopped chopping the wood with me. All he did now was cut down the trees and then we would drag the logs closer to the house where I then had to chop it into firewood. Every week he dragged me to the dump with him. While no one was around to watch, he would hunt for items he could transform for his own purposes. He had an old, beat up pickup truck which he used for hauling his so-called treasures. When we first moved in the woods my father had found an old wood stove and this is how we cooked our meals, the old fashion way. I had to make dinner as my mother refused to cook. But even if my mother had tried, she was always so drunk everything would have burnt, including the house. It was not worth letting her cook. I had also learned to drive the pickup truck before I was thirteen because often on the way back my father was so inebriated I had to drive back home. He never left the, so-called, house without a six-pack of beer, which he drank non-stop.

They usually slept all day, waking only around four o'clock in the afternoon. This routine of theirs allowed me to slip away. If I wasn't in the house when they woke, they simply assumed I was in the woods working on the firewood or something of the sort. In reality, I spent my days in Sault Ste. Marie, the closest city to Echo Bay. Mornings, I spent at the Bayliss Public Library and I worked part-time as a cleaning lady at the Mid-City Motel on East Portage Avenue. I worked under an alias and made sure I was paid cash to avoid being traced later, after I ran away, because that was my plan all along. This plan was the only thing that kept me alive and hopeful for many years. My job only occupied half my day, my shift started at eleven every morning, Monday to Friday, and ended around two in the afternoon. My only means of transportation was a local school bus that stopped on the main road at seven forty five every morning. From the Sault Ste. Marie High School drop off, I went directly to the library and studied all morning until my shift started. Luckily the motel was only a few blocks from both the library and the school. I also made sure I was back at the bus stop before the end of the school day. Echo Bay was too far to walk.

I spent all my spare time at the library. I watched the students and studied the same books they did. This was the only way I could get an education because there was no way my drunken parents would allow me to go to school. I never brought any books home. First of all I did not have a library card but no one knew, and secondly I didn't want my parents to know what I was up to while they were sleeping off the booze, getting ready for their next intoxication.

The bus ride was forty-five minutes long, with all the stops, which allowed a lot of time for daydreaming. Most of the time it was the same daydream over and over. I dreamt of getting away from my parents, sooner rather than later. Every day I went through the same routine of going to the library, going to work and coming back. For a long time, I planned this escape from my horrible life. I knew that somewhere there was a better life, somewhere there was pride, and joy, and laughter. Sometimes I heard music and was overwhelmed with a sensation of wellbeing. Music seemed to run through me and made my body itch to move to the beat. Of course I never did because whenever I heard music I was in a public place.

Freedom seemed so far away, yet I could still perceive the day I would feel free. I spent hours dreaming of my imminent freedom.

I worked hard every day at the hotel to save every dollar that I made. Every moment I spent in Sault Ste. Marie not working I spent at the library studying. Studying very hard, knowing that one day that knowledge would be useful to me. Somehow this knowledge would be part of the key to my freedom.

On the bus I scarcely spoke with other students. I was not only shy about talking with them but I knew they would ask questions. Therefore in order not to have to answer any of those questions I simply stared out the window and watched the scenery go by. Watching the trees change along with the seasons. In the summer, when the school bus stopped doing its run, I biked back and forth. I had found a bike during one of the runs at the junk yard. With the help of cycling magazines and books from the library, I managed to identify and find - also during junkyard hunts - the parts required to fix it. This only gave me time to work at the motel but it was better than nothing.

As eager as I was on the way to Sault Ste. Marie in the morning I dreaded the return home. I hated going back, I hated the fact that I would be yelled at and told to make dinner with the nothings contained in this grungy weathered log house: my parents' home. I dreamt of the day I would have my own home. It would be a beautiful modern place with contemporary furniture. The decor would be streamlined. I hated clutter and that's all I seemed to have around me in my parents' home, stinky clutter. Sometimes at the library I would look at some home decor magazines and daydream some more. As I looked at all the new modern furniture styles, which were the current trends, I would imagine almost exactly how I would set up my own living room, dining room, kitchen, I even knew the type of dishes and cutlery I wished to have. As for my bedroom it would be a very private and distinguished area. I didn't care about having a large place, I just wanted a place of my own that I could furnish and decorate in my own style. Every time I looked at those magazines it just added more details to my imagined future home and life.

I wanted to be my own person and somehow I felt the hard lessons learned from my parents would be useful to me in the future. I promised myself that I would never treat my own children - if I ever decided to have children - the same way my parents had treated me.

I dreamed of becoming an important businesswoman when I was older. I wanted to be recognized across the world. I knew I would never be the kind of woman that would depend on a man. I also knew life would not be easy, or kind to me. My father had always told me that I was a "plain Jane", not pretty enough to attract a decent guy. But I was never interested in marrying. I was not the kind to go after a guy. And I definitely did not want to marry a poor, lazy jerk like my father. I had seen too much of what these were made of. All I had to do was look at my parents. I had seen the unhappiness, lack of money, lack love, and lack respect.

I knew money was not the key to true happiness, but I still wanted to be rich when I got older. The wealth would be achieved from my own work and I would live on my own terms. I had slaved for my parents long enough I was not going to be somebody else's slave again.

Younger, I had dreamt of becoming a model but from repeatedly hearing my father say that I was a "plain Jane", I knew that modeling was out of the question. So I tried to focus on a different career path. I was not sure exactly what I wanted to do yet but I had a few different ideas. Photographer was one, I also dreamt of becoming an archaeologist. I wanted to do something that would allow me to travel the world.

Every other night I went to the Laundromat to wash some clothes. This served two purposes, first and foremost to get away from my parents and secondly to contain the amount of laundry to be done at one time, keeping the quantity of clothes to lug around at a minimum.

The cave, in which I hid that night of June 17, 2004, was large enough for me to move around in a crouched position. I dug out the hidden backpack from behind some branches in the corner. Took it out of its' sealed plastic garbage bag and started changing into my new identity. Strapped to my body was close to thirty thousand dollars in cash I had saved up over the last three years. I lodged a small mirror on a rock and started to cut my long hair slightly shorter to better hide it under my baseball cap. The glow from the flash light wasn't great but it would have to do. I put on a baseball cap and some glasses in order to make sure the few people I knew did not recognize me. Everything I needed was stashed in this cave or on my body, prepared for the split second that would change my life forever.

Morning didn't come quick enough. I was so eager to leave this forsaken town, so few people knew me making it easier to slip away unnoticed. And now with this new look and name, no one would ever guess it was me. An old Toyota, I had purchased the month before, was waiting for me at the end of the trail with a full tank of gas. You couldn't tell it was there unless you were looking for it. Its dark green paint helped with this camouflage. It was that quality that attracted me to the car. I was so thankful I had bought this vehicle. Had I snapped over a month ago I would have been traveling by foot or bike, but I didn't have to worry about that now.

When day finally broke, it was a beautiful sunny one at least that's how I saw it. Long awaited freedom can make even a rainy day look beautifully sunny, but it actually was a bright sunny morning. Not a cloud in the sky. "This must be a sign," I thought to myself.

I drove west on highway seventeen, smiling to myself the whole way. I felt as if a huge weight had been lifted from my shoulders. I could finally breathe. A new beginning was on the horizon, a fresh start. The winding road ahead felt peaceful, a feeling I had never experienced before. It felt really good. The beauty of the mountains ahead, the evergreens each side of the road and the view of the lake on my left all held a whole new world just for me. For the first time in my life I was able to savour what I saw. Tears of joy ran down my cheeks and butterflies fluttered in my stomach.

By dinnertime I finally arrived at my destination. My legs felt slightly numb as I got out of my car. Yes, my car. I still couldn't believe I had taken control of my life leaving everything behind, everything and everyone, especially the pain. My new life was waiting. I couldn't wait to get started on this new life I had planned for the last three years. I spent three years thinking and carefully planning this particular day. The day I would leave the confines of a painful, demeaning, and insecure life I had endured too long. Now, I had finally reached the light at the end of the tunnel. I was so ready for this new beginning. A scream of joy and laughter just spilt out of me.

Earlier that day, as Christa had rushed out the door, a candle fell into the curtains instantly turning them into a torch. It did not take long before the house was completely engulfed. Flames were blazing out of the windows. The roof had already collapsed as the firemen made their way up to the house. They were too late to salvage anything.

Residents of the town had noticed smoke hovering above the forest. The fire truck had followed a dirt trail from the main road.

Two firemen tore down the door and rushed into the house.

"Larry! I think we're too late," he pointed at the inert body laying on what seemed to have been a couch at one time and another laying face down on the floor. They each grabbed a body, got out of the burning house, and carried them to the paramedics who had just reached the scene. But there was no pulse on either and they were both pronounced D.O.A.

The firemen finally got the blaze under control. The investigators then started their search for the cause of the fire. Several hours later, the officials declared the fire to be accidental. The investigation ended there.

They looked for identification in order to contact the next of kin but they only found the woman's coordinates. When they ran her name through the system the only relative found was a sister in Chicago.

"Hello?" A sophisticated voice answered the phone.

"May I speak to Rebecca Reese?" Detective Constable Clark inquired on the other end of the line.

"This is she," the woman replied obviously waiting to know what this was all about.

"Ms. Reese, I'm sorry to have to tell you this over the phone. We have unfortunate news about your sister, Mrs. Sara Makins." Constable Clark hated giving bad news.

"What did she do this time?" The voice was no longer soft. It suddenly became apprehensive which both rattled and shocked Constable Clark.

"She hasn't done anything, ma'am. She died." He blurted out in reflex of his annoyance to her reaction.

"Oh! My God! I'm sorry if I sounded insensitive Officer but she always used to get in trouble and drag me into it. Obviously that didn't build a solid relationship between us. How did it happen?" Constable Clark could hear the mortification in her voice.

"They died in a fire. The house completely burnt down."

"All three of them?" A trace of concern could be detected in her voice.

"Why do you say all three of them, Ms. Reese? We only found two bodies," this raised a red flag for Constable Clark. "The other body was of a man but we could not find any identification in the house. We were hoping you could enlighten us as to who he was."

"His name was Hank Makins. You couldn't find identification for him because he was a bum, nothing more, nothing less." Disdain transpired through her words. "So, where is my niece? Should I come pick her up?"

Constable Clark was confused by the question. "I'm afraid there is no trace of your niece, ma'am. Are you sure she lived with them?"

As soon as Constable Clarke ended his conversation with Ms. Makins, he urgently called the fire department.

"Larry? This is Constable Clark. We need to search the Makins house again. The sister says there was a seventeen year old living there."

"Are you sure?" Larry was stunned by the statement. The house had shown no trace of anyone other than the deceased ever having lived there.

"I'm also putting a missing person's report out. We need to find this young girl A.S.A.P!"

FIRST DAY OF SCHOOL

Lakehead University is located in the middle of Thunder Bay. Thunder Bay is a small city in the Northern part of Ontario, Canada with a population of 117,000. It is located at the tip of Lake Superior, bordered from the south by the state of Michigan, USA further west you end up in Manitoba, Canada and North is just endless Canadian forest. One could easily hide and never be found in this part of the world.

Dale and Brooke, twin brothers, escaped here hoping to become invisible to the rest of the world. Dale had mastered being so ordinary that people usually forgot him the second he was out of sight. So much so, he usually had to re-introduce himself several times before a person actually remembered him. His first day at Lakehead, he applied his usual charm.

"Good morning class. Those that are here for Mathematics 1160, stay. Others please leave immediately so we may proceed with our agenda," was Ms. Hamilton's opening statement. She seemed very straight forward. One could tell she had been teaching for quite a while.

He sat in the far back corner of the class to avoid having anyone behind him. He always had to see the whole room. It bothered him to have people behind him or out of his sight. He could not explain the reasons for this behaviour and actually never tried. Instinctively, he always placed himself in a position to see everything. He needed a clear view of the doorway and everyone surrounding him.

This first year of University, he knew would not be easy but he was focused. Most people would qualify him as a 'geek'. His twin brother, Brooke, on the other hand was more of a social butterfly. He liked to go out and meet friends. He managed to work part time and had absolutely no interest in studies. He came with Dale for the company but also because they never parted, they had a very special bond despite the fact that they were complete opposites. They had matching features but dressed and styled their hair so differently that most people did not realize they were identical twins. Their differences extended beyond mere physicalities; they also had complete opposite personalities. One seemed to complement the other.

Their parents were lost in their own little drunken world and they had no other relatives to speak of. So it was really no big deal for anyone when they decided to move to Thunder Bay. Actually, no one really noticed when they left.

"Hi! I'm Geneva," a voice tore Dale from his thoughts, as everyone walked out of class, "and you are," she, not so subtly, inquired. The hallway was crowded with students walking to and fro. It felt kind of claustrophobic to Dale.

"Oh? Hi, Geneva. I'm Dale." He said with much embarrassment. He never knew how to handle these situations. Moments like this he wished he was the 'Invisible Man'. He could barely look her in the eyes from fear she would notice his discomfort.

"Are you from around here?" she continued.

"No, I just moved here in June," he answered.

"Me too!" she said. "If you ever want to join me in exploring the city, let me know. Gotta run! See ya next class. Oh! Before I go, here's my number," Geneva handed him a folded piece of paper and turned away. She had mesmerizing green eyes hidden behind heavy black framed glasses. Her skin was fair and free of any type of make-up. Long wavy auburn hair framed her angelic face. She was almost as tall as he was. Her body was very slim, almost boyish, and slightly athletic.

Dale felt really nervous and could only mutter; "Thanks," but it was too late. Geneva had already left by the time he snapped out of it. As Dale walked to his next class, the recent events were racing through his mind. He simply did not know how to react towards girls. The rest of the day went without further disruptions. He avoided eye contact going from class to class. He kept his head down when crossing paths with others. The only people he actually looked at were his teachers during class. At lunchtime, he found a quiet corner and simply reviewed his notes and books while he ate. He spread his books around him to discourage anyone from sitting close to him and it worked.

Walking back home he was satisfied with how cleverly he avoided further contact but that incident with that Geneva chick still lingered in his mind. He hoped that his indifferent and unsociable behaviour would put her off.

As usual, after dinner Brooke went out. Every night was the same; Brooke would go out socializing with his friends. Four days a week, he worked as a bartender at the Voo-Doo Lounge, making enough money to support both of them while Dale studied.

Brooke worked nights and slept during the day. Dale went to school during the day and slept at night. This made it easier to live in a one-bedroom house. They shared the same room and bed but with their different schedules they actually never interacted. Although they had been brought up in the same household their views of the world were completely opposite. They didn't agree on anything. Yet, they were inseparable, not in the spending time together way because they never did that, but they could never part ways. Where ever one went the other always followed. Anything that happened to one also happened to the other.

They chose to come to Thunder Bay partly because of the University but mostly because it was a remote city. One could easily be invisible in this part of the country. They didn't want to attract too much attention. Identical twins usually did, which is why they thought Thunder Bay might be the place for them. It provided Dale with great education facilities and Brooke was able to find a job easily.

The tiny house they rented was located on Andrew Street. It was a very quiet area; most residents on that street were retired folks. The house was already furnished with the basics. A futon style couch accompanied by an end table and a small black and white television jacked up on an old style television stand occupied the living room. The couch was the only relatively recent item in the house. In the middle of the kitchen stood a sixties style dinning set. The tabletop was silver speckled yellow linoleum and the chair seats and backrests were covered in yellow vinyl. Both table and chairs were trimmed with a silver plastic band and chrome studs. Amazingly, this dinning set still looked brand new. The appliances were as old as the furniture but still did the job. The bedroom was scarcely furnished with a twin size bed and a four-drawer dresser. The bathroom was pretty standard with a white cast iron bathtub, white china toilet and sink dropped into a simple cabinet painted white. The floor was baby blue ceramic mosaic tile, the walls were covered with four-inch square tiles of the same light blue colour, and a black ceramic tile border edged the top and each end of the tub area. All the walls were painted white and the floors were heavily varnished hardwood flooring, Maple to be precise. The finish had yellowed with the years giving the floors a honey colour. The place had not been decorated since the sixties but was very clean. Brooke and Dale didn't need anything more. The rent was affordable and the owner was a nice retired couple. They were very amiable but kept to themselves which the twins greatly appreciated. The last thing they wanted were landlords that drop by all the time and snoop around their business.

They didn't add anything to the decor. They liked its' simplicity. They didn't have any photographs or personal trinkets to add. They didn't watch much television so the black and white version was fine with the few channels that came in via antenna. They also didn't want to spend too much money until Dale was done University. They were very strict with their budget. They had saved a bit of money before they came to Thunder Bay. This money they tried not to spend. They were saving it for a rainy day. Brooke made enough money at the Voo-Doo Lounge to support them comfortably. They ate well and did not have many expenses. Their rent included utilities and Dale had paid his full tuition for the year. He was not a fashion buff so very little money was spent on clothes and he never went out.

Every week Brooke handed his pay to Dale and kept the tips for his own expenses. Dale never asked how much Brooke made in tips, or how much he spent. He preferred not to know. Brooke made the money so Dale didn't feel he had the right to ask.

Brooke usually met with his friends for a few hours before going into work, and on his nights off they often went to the Voo-Doo Lounge anyway for a few drinks after seeing a movie or doing some activity or other. But they always had the same discussion of 'what should we do?' and the conclusion more often than not was the same night after night.

Everyone was waiting for him at Starbucks on Memorial Avenue. They always met at the same place, usually sat at the same table and each had an unspoken, assigned seat. From there they planned the rest of their evening.

"We were starting to wonder if you were coming," blurted Gregory. He was Brooke's best buddy along with Josh and Peter. Brooke had met them while working at the Voo-Doo Lounge. Greg and Brooke had hit it off instantly and whoever was a friend of Greg was also a friend of Peter and Josh.

Greg was a tall skinny guy with short brown curly hair, brown eyes and his skin had an olive tint to it. Peter was slightly shorter than Greg at five eleven. He had blond hair to his shoulders, his eyes were green and his skin was the colour of milk. Josh was about the same height as Peter, and his skin was also as white as Peter's but his hair was dark brown styled in a fashionable bed head chic. His eyes were clear blue and sometimes it almost felt like he could see right through you, which sometimes made people uncomfortable.

As much as Greg and Brooke got along, Josh disliked Brooke but kept that to himself and respected the friendship with Greg. Josh had a feeling that Brooke was not what he claimed to be. Something was odd about him and Josh was keeping an eye out for his friend. One day Brooke would show his true colours and Josh would be there to see them.

"You guys know what it's like," the frustration could easily be read on Brooke's face. The guys already knew how he was supporting his brother and himself. His brother Dale was attending Lakehead University leaving Brooke with large financial responsibilities or so they thought. They figured that this kind of responsibility was a lot of pressure for an eighteen year old.

"So what's the plan?" Peter was always anxious to get going. He hated to waste time. Ironically, they never did anything important. They simply hung out at different places.

"Relax Pete!" Brooke had no patience for Peter's fretfulness, "I just got here."

"Well, we've been waiting for over half an hour," Peter didn't intend on putting up with Brooke's moodiness.

"Fine! What did you guys discuss while you were waiting?"

"We were debating between the Lounge and seeing a movie." Gregory answered more calmly than Peter had.

"Which is the preference?" Brooke asked. He calmed his tone down too. He knew the boys well enough not to provoke further disruption.

"Well, Peter and I prefer the Lounge and Josh was suggesting a movie," Gregory was usually the case presenter. Being Brooke's best friend, the guys thought Greg had the best chance at getting Brooke to agree to their preference.

"Then let's go to the Lounge," Brooke quickly responded. "I could use a drink."

They all got up and left without one more word. They were not a very talkative group. But neither minded the silence. Some people would have said that they seemed to communicate without having to open their mouths. Sometimes just a look gave the others all the info they needed.

At the Voo-Doo Lounge everyone knew them and even the bartender, working opposite nights to Brooke, seemed to understand their silent language. Brooke normally sipped on his drink until they were ready to leave. He never drank much. Gregory and the others on the other hand, usually, made it worthwhile for the bartender. They never drove which was a relief but had they needed a designated driver, they could have always counted on Brooke. Gregory always thought it odd how Brooke seemed so controversial; part of him was quite wild, while the other was quite tame. His looks and attitude reflected a big city boy but on the other hand he would throw them off with slight considerate actions. His light drinking was one of those conservative sides of his character. While his bark was as loud as the worst of them, his drinking reminded that of a woman, stretching a drink almost the whole evening. He would be out all night but was never late for work. Meeting his friends was a different story; he was always late for that. He always took care of looking his best; he never had a hair out of place. The other odd point about Brooke was his extensive knowledge. Especially considering how young and uneducated he was. He could talk about pretty much anything with some knowledge of it, which was usually more than the average person. Gregory knew there was more to Brooke than met the eye. He kept a keen sight on him trying to figure Brooke out but he tended to be evasive and introverted. His friends almost seemed to be a front for him, a way of hiding behind a shield. Brooke didn't speak much but he listened very attentively until someone started repeating themselves, then boredom could easily be read on his face. He would start looking around the room and twitch on his chair, changing positions every ten seconds or less.

His face was very expressive this was probably the most revealing part of his character, if not the only. If one spent enough time observing Brooke they could see that his brain never shut down. He always seemed to be thinking about something or other. But no one really knew him, not deep down. He didn't let anyone in. Greg often wondered why. He had a feeling Brooke hid something painful deep inside. What? Greg could not begin to imagine. Brooke never gave an inkling of a clue. Sometimes Gregory would try to dig with some small talk. He tried to bring up different subjects that might get Brooke to open up but nothing had yet broken the mystery behind his friend.

Every now and then one or more of the guys had a girlfriend. Sometimes the girlfriend would tag along but in the four months that Greg had known Brooke he never heard of or saw him with a girlfriend. It wasn't because he couldn't find one. At work he had a flock of girls fighting for his attention. Some of them were as bold as to ask him out but Brooke always declined. Whenever Greg asked him about it, he simply brushed it off saying he had no interest. He said he was too busy, and didn't have time for this crap. Oddly, Brooke often tried to push the persistent ones onto Greg.

THE NEXT DAY

The next morning, as Dale locked the door to the house Brooke and he rented, he felt a light tap on his shoulder. Startled, he turned abruptly almost knocking Geneva to the ground.

"Oh my God! I'm so sorry Geneva," he said as he saw her. His face turned crimson. "Are you all right?"

Geneva stared at him, eyes wide with surprise and fear. She looked as if she had just encountered an evil being. He felt like she saw right through him. It was as if she could read the secrets he tried so hard to hide. "Really, I'm sorry. I didn't hear you come." He hoped she would say something. "You startled me. I'm really sorry. Please, stop staring at me that way and say something." He pleaded.

"I'm fine." She hesitated to say then looked down to straighten her clothes. Then she looked up again. "I saw you as I walked out of my house. I live just across the street. See? That house there," she pointed toward a plain looking, two story white clapboard house with dark blue shutters directly in front of Dale's residence, "I thought we could probably walk to campus together." She smiled at him. He was relieved to see the fear had completely disappeared from her eyes.

He didn't know how to say no, so he simply fell into step with her. Inside, he was struggling to find a way of getting out of this situation. He had a feeling this was just the beginning and that Geneva would expect them to walk together every day. He brushed his flattened hair nervously with his free hand as he walked. He wondered why Geneva kept coming up to him. He knew he was not the type of guy to attract any attention. He wore conservative clothing, mostly beige, brown, or grey in colour. He wore his hair flat on his head separated to one side and the cheapest and ugliest eyeglasses money could buy. He did nothing to attract girls. Just then his glasses slipped right off his nose and onto the sidewalk. He clumsily picked them up and quickly put them back on. Luckily they hadn't broken but he was so embarrassed. Could things get any worst for him? Geneva just stood patiently looking the other way as to not embarrass him more than he already was. Then she simply fell into step with him when he had regained control of the situation. At no time did she laugh or make any jokes about the situation. This surprised him very much. This girl had class. Then, as if nothing had happened, she started making conversation again.

"So Dale, what other courses are you taking? I haven't seen you in any other classes of mine." Geneva was full of positive energy. She simply smiled all the time and her eyes seemed to light up when she looked at him, causing him to regress even more. He did not want to feel so comfortable around her. It seemed way too easy to become friends with her. He was a loner. He didn't want friends.

"I'm taking a Major in Geoarchaeology. What about you?" Geneva made conversation so easy, making it even harder for him to find excuses to get away from her.

"Wow! That must be really interesting. I'm studying Mechanical Engineering. Following in my Dad's footsteps," she responded with a smile. For a moment she almost looked shy.

"That sounds pretty interesting too."

"Actually it is," Geneva explained how she was learning all the different functions and movements, reactions, wear and tear, and influence of different materials. It was pretty interesting to hear her talk. She was very passionate about the subject.

As they continued walking, they talked about the different courses their respective fields required and before Dale knew it they were in class ready to start another day.

During lunch, Geneva sought Dale out but he hid to avoid her. He felt rather cheap as he watched her walking around looking for him. He couldn't understand what a beautiful, intelligent girl like her could possibly want with him. He wished she would just forget he existed but at the same time he surprised himself feeling kind of flattered and enjoying her attention. These mixed feelings really put him in turmoil. So much so, that he had to run to the restroom room to puke his guts out.

As he came out of the stall, one guy looked at him with a frown and mumbled; "What are you, a girl?" Then he simply walked out keeping his frown and eyes on Dale. Dale quickly washed up and walked out, head low. He felt so uneasy. He nervously kept flattening his already flat hair with his free hand. He didn't like drawing attention to himself, yet since he had walked into Lakehead it seemed everything he did drew attention, so much for trying to be invisible. He successfully avoided Geneva the rest of the day. Even if she was interesting, he still didn't want to let her into his life.

When he got home he did some schoolwork, ate and as usual by seven thirty Brooke was out the door.

BROOKE AT WORK

Brooke didn't have any official bartending training but having lived with alcoholic parents all his life, he had a natural knack for the job. He knew how these lushes thought and what they wanted. His boss, Jim, gave him a chance at the job after much pleading from Brooke and had not regretted it. Brooke had only worked at the Voo-Doo Lounge a few months but was already the most popular bartender in the place.

He attracted a crowd every night he worked. He really knew how to work people. He made every customer feel special and Jim liked to watch. He had never met a bartender so in tune with his crowd. Brooke was like a rock star with faithful groupies. It was beautiful. The girls practically threw themselves at him and the guys all wanted to be his buddy, which was strange considering Brooke's effeminate looks. But somehow Brooke managed to make them feel like every single one of them was special to him. He would joke around with them, compliment the women and talk shop with the guys. They just couldn't get enough of him. Brooke also had an amazing memory. Miraculously he remembered every name and everything each one of them told him. After only a few times of seeing someone he would have their drink prepared before they even asked. People loved that. He always asked them pertinent questions. If someone had mentioned an interview, the following time he saw him or her he inquired about it. If another mentioned a birth or sickness in the family again he would follow up with this person during their next visit. Jim was amazed by Brooke's ways with his customers. He was actually considering making Brooke his right hand man.

Brooke was also a very responsible bartender. He would never let his customers get smashed. He stopped selling them alcoholic drinks when he saw they had enough, even if they got persistent. Brooke would give them a glass of pop, mineral water or even coffee before allowing them to have another drink or leaving. Strangely enough, sales were better than they ever had been.

Since Brooke had been hired, business had increased considerably. Jim was finally making a profit and no longer considered selling the place. He was at last starting to feel the way he thought he would when he had first decided to open the joint. His dreams were finally coming true.

Jim was a man without a family and this place was his love child. He had ventured into it without prior experience and with all his savings. He had even sold his house to finance this project. Until Brooke came along he had started to regret the move but now things were starting to feel like it had been worth the sacrifices.

Jim was grateful to have Brooke around and knew deep down he should show him his appreciation. He sensed that Brooke had not had an easy life; therefore any break would be welcome. Brooke never spoke of his personal life with Jim or anyone else for that matter. But Jim could see it in the kid's eyes. As young as Brooke was, his eyes told a different story. The kid's eyes were more mature than his age.

Jim wanted to wait until Brooke had been employed for a full year and then he was going to make him a business proposition. In the meantime, he would take him under his wing and make sure Brooke was happy at work and everywhere else. He almost felt like he could be a father figure to this kid. Jim didn't have children because he had been too busy living a wild life. Before the Lounge he had enjoyed himself. The house he had sold to finance his business had belonged to his parents. He inherited it when they passed away. The Lounge was his way of grounding himself and the only commitment he was willing to make. Jim had never married or settled down with anyone because he never wanted to hurt another person. If the Lounge hadn't worked out well he would be the only one to endure the consequences. Now Brooke was awakening a protective side Jim never knew existed within him. He wanted to cut the kid a well-deserved break.

A FRIENDSHIP DEVELOPS

About a month into the semester, as Dale walked towards his second period class he heard footsteps running behind him. Just as he turned around to see what it was all about, he heard Geneva calling. He had managed to avoid her most mornings by leaving after watching her go and giving her a head start of few blocks. She had knocked on his door a few of these mornings but he never answered the door. Now she was haunting him again.

"Dale!" Everyone turned to look, his face turned blood red. This one always gave him colours whether he wanted them or not.

"Oh! Hi Geneva," he responded hoping to stop the stares. What did this girl want with him? Why couldn't she just leave him alone as everyone else did? Almost every single day that past month Geneva sought him out and tried to make friendly conversation. She just couldn't take a hint even if you spelled it out for her. Most days he had been able to avoid her. It hadn't been easy because she was very persistent and clever. Whenever she caught him off guard Dale had spoken to her out of politeness. He wasn't big on being rude. He didn't like hurting peoples' feelings. He guessed that he never made it clear enough to her that he didn't really want a friendship.

"I was hoping to catch you. What are you doing Saturday? I thought we might go sightseeing." She had a huge smile on her face. She looked as if she was going to burst with joy. Dale could only wonder how someone could possibly look so happy. He wondered if she had swallowed fireworks when she was a kid or something. He imagined a giant needle bursting her bubble. Pop!

"I can't. I have to study," that was the best he could come up with, hoping she would finally get the drift. A lame excuse he thought was a sure way of giving someone a hint. Pop!

"Oh!" she responded looking painfully disappointed and then she looked up all bubbly again, "Maybe I could help you study?" It was amazing how quickly she could bounce back to her bubbly self. She must have an unlimited supply of soap up her wazoo.

"I don't think so. My folks don't want any strangers in the house." Pop!

Geneva looked totally puzzled at that response. "Don't you live alone with your brother?"

"Yes, but when we left our folks warned us about having people over." She could see right through his lies.

"And how would they know?" attempted Geneva.

"I'd rather not deceive them," Dale was getting annoyed and wanted to end this conversation. Giant needle. Pop!

"Well, maybe some other time then," Geneva said and finally ran off. She always came and went like the wind. Dale couldn't help thinking that if there was a way of taking those Energizer batteries out of her he sure would like to know. Her high energy was more than he could handle.

He made it to his next class avoiding eye contact with anyone. He always kept his head low. The down side to this was sometimes bumping into people, literally, but he just didn't like seeing the stares. He always felt like people looked at him as if he were an alien or something. The incident with Geneva kept taunting him. He surprised himself feeling bad about the way he had turned her away. Worst, he realized he actually liked her and would have liked to spend Saturday with her. Grumpy, in him, was starting to wear off. Why was he so scared of everything and everyone anyway? He started to wonder. He knew that after this incident Geneva would probably never speak to him again. He had probably really busted her bubble with his imaginary giant needle. So, he decided to find her during lunch to apologize.

Lunch came and went but he couldn't find Geneva anywhere. He searched all the usual spots he had observed her hanging about, and generally avoided, but nothing. After his last class he waited at the exit doors, where she usually came out. He never saw Geneva emerge. On his way home he decided to stop by her house but lost his nerve. Once he got home the usual routine set in. He stayed in and Brooke went out.

The next morning he got up earlier so he wouldn't miss Geneva on the way to campus. He watched from the window for her to come out but the time came where he absolutely had to leave. They had a class together that day but she didn't attend. He really started to feel like she was now avoiding him. Now, that he wanted to speak to her she was nowhere to be found. He knew it was his fault. The guilt was eating at him.

All day he kept an eye out for her but nothing. He knew he had to build the courage to walk up to her house. Which he did before going home that day but he had not built enough nerve to knock on the door. 'I'm such a wimp,' he thought.

The next day came and still no Geneva. This was now the third day and he was really getting worried. That was a new feeling for him, never before had he ever worried about anyone. His worry about Geneva got him concerned about what was happening to him. The last thing he wanted was to get too close to anyone and vice-versa. This situation was really getting to him. Dale decided that he would check-up on Geneva and once he knew she was fine he would then keep his distance.

After his last class this third day he rang Geneva's doorbell. A woman, he assumed to be Geneva's mother, opened the door.

"Can I help you, young man?" she said with a smile. 'Young man', it always felt funny to hear someone call him that.

"Yes, Ma'am, I would simply like to know if everything is alright with Geneva. I haven't seen her on campus in the last few days." It took all his courage to muster these two sentences. He kept his head down, looking at his shoes, steeling a glance at the old lady every now and then. The smell of homemade cooking was overpowering and made his stomach growl. He hoped she didn't hear. He was embarrassed enough as it was.

"Oh! How nice of you. Yes, she is fine. Just a little flu but she should be back on her feet and back in class by Monday. Who shall I tell her called?"

"No one!" He huffed in a panic. Then added; "Thank you. Please don't tell her I came. I really just wanted to make sure she was okay." On these last words he turned around and ran home across the street. He felt like such a dope. Why hadn't he just left it alone? He knew that if Geneva knew he called on her she would simply be encouraged to pursue him further. Why hadn't he just left it alone?

The weekend zipped by. Monday morning Dale heard a knock on his door. When he opened it, Geneva was standing there all smiles. He couldn't help but smile back. Seeing her this way made his heart melt. Her cheerfulness was almost contagious. He was letting his guards down. Until that moment he had still worried about her without even realizing it. Seeing her back to her normal self lifted a weight off his shoulders. He was still uneasy with getting too close but he thought it was time to take a chance on friendship.

"Are you ready yet," she inquired.

"Just let me get my coat," He ran inside got his coat and backpack. "I saw you Friday from my bedroom window," she said loud enough for him to hear. "Mrs. Anderson said you were worried."

"I'm sorry about the other day," he started to say. "I wanted to apologize."

"Ah! Don't worry about it. I understand we haven't known each other that long. But I still would like to go sightseeing with you," Geneva replied before he could even say anything further.

"I would really like that too," he chanced. How bad could it be? It's not like this was a marriage proposal or anything, besides it would probably do him good to get out a little. Friendship was something new for Dale and he thought it was probably time he took a crack at it. "So how bad was that flu? What happened," he asked her.

She then explained how it suddenly hit her during her second class and had to rush home. Some other students in one of her classes the previous day had been sick. She assumed that was most likely where she had caught the virus. She had spent four days in bed on a liquid diet and lost five pounds. She was already quite skinny and really did not need to lose those pounds.

Their conversation diversified as they walked to Lakehead and he knew then and there that Geneva and he were meant to be good friends. She wasn't like other girls that he saw around campus, giggling about cute guys smiling at them or snubbing the 'uncool' kids, like him. Geneva was real. She had a style of her own and made geeky look good. Geneva wasn't cheerleader material, but if you looked closely, she was beautiful in a genuine way.

As they walked to campus every now and then Geneva would point out something. It could be anything from the shape of a tree that was slightly out of the ordinary to the way a squirrel was shelling a nut. She noticed everything around her and her fascination was almost childlike. She never pointed out the same thing twice. It was really cute the way she looked at everything with untainted eyes. Sometimes Dale wondered if she hadn't been kept in a cage most of her life.

He couldn't help thinking, so much for taking his distances with her. But every time he was around Geneva he felt like a completely different person. Dale tried to resent and resist Geneva's friendship but her charm was stronger. Her presence was intoxicating. The more time he spent with her the more he wanted to be around her. Somehow when he was around her he forgot the world around them. When they talked, it was as if only the two of them existed. Dale had never felt anything like it before. He usually was alone in his bubble. Never before had he let anyone in. He felt really bad about having been such a jerk before.

The next morning Geneva was knocking on the front door as Dale was putting his jacket on. A flash of excitement ran through him at the sound of her knock. He hadn't realized it until then that he had been eager to see her again. He had enjoyed her company to and from campus the previous day. Subconsciously, he had been looking forward to morning. This new friendship was better than he ever would have imagined.

"So, Dale, what have you seen so far in Thunder Bay?" she started.

"Nothing, I've been too busy with classes and studying." Dale answered a little embarrassed. He realized then how cooped up he had been. Dale had arrived in Thunder Bay about two and a half months before classes started but had spent all his time preparing for the upcoming session. It had not taken long to find a place and settle in. The place was already furnished and they, Brooke and he, only had a little bit of clothing. They had not brought anything more. No souvenirs or pictures of any sort. They had left everything behind in hopes of a fresh start and they also didn't want to be bogged down with dragging useless trinkets around.

"Oh! Well, you have got to get out more," she said laughing. "From now on I will personally take charge of your social education." She continued to giggle as she said it in a 'meant-to-be serious' tone.

"Are you sure you're up to the challenge?" Dale followed also laughing. Geneva's laugh was quite addictive. He was surprised at how comfortable she made him feel. Although they had just started hanging out together less than a week before, it felt as if they had known each other all their lives.

"By the way, your mom seems like a nice lady," Dale commented.

"My mom," Geneva inquired, her face turning into a grimace. He had never seen her frown before.

He reminded her that he had inquired about her when she was sick. Her eyes lit up with sudden understanding.

"That's not my mom." Geneva then went on to explaining that she rented a room from Mrs. Anderson. Her family lived in the boonies up north, they had no idea she was here, and she wanted to keep it that way. She had run away at the beginning of summer and had not advised anyone about her whereabouts. She was a single child and had no uncles, aunts or grandparents.

"I thought we could start planning our sightseeing trip as we walk together." She quickly changed the subject. At that moment Dale noticed that Geneva was holding a stack of brochures.

"I thought you already had a plan," he said teasing her. She laughed and admitted that she did but wanted to run it by him first.

"I didn't want to look too pushy by imposing it on you." She was wearing her everlasting smile. Dale couldn't help wondering if her cheeks ever got sore or tired from all that smiling.

"I know I'm probably taking a huge risk," he continued to tease, "but I am prepared to trust you for one day."

"Good. Only one thing, do you have access to a car?" She looked down at the sidewalk as she asked. She looked a little embarrassed. This amused him. Dale didn't think Geneva could ever get embarrassed; she always seemed so in control.

"Actually, I do. My landlord lets me park my car in the garage behind the house." Dale was happy he could contribute.

As they walked she handed him one brochure at a time, explaining what she thought might be interesting to visit and why. Dale was fascinated by how much research she had done on all these sites.

Every day that week they walked to and from campus together. Geneva usually was knocking on Dale's door before he got a chance to walk out. He quickly discovered that she was a very punctual and organized girl. During their walks, they discovered that they had many things in common. They both enjoyed reading the same type of books and despised the same authors. Dale was amazed to find someone he could relate to so easily. Something about Geneva made him feel good about himself. That too was a new feeling for him. Growing up, his parents had put him down every day. They continuously told him he was stupid, lazy, and ugly. They always told him that he would never amount to much, not to kid himself into thinking that he would do any better than they had. Those comments alone had actually fuelled his desire to do better, but sometimes Dale would fall into a dark mood and believe everything they had told him. He continuously fought with both sides, even now far away from them. Some days he felt like he could conquer the world and other days he felt like hiding in the bottom of a cave for the rest of his life. These moods were unpredictable but in public, Dale always tried to look positive. He didn't want anyone to see his vulnerability.

Being around Geneva made Dale feel like he was on top of a mountain, everything looked different; the air felt fresher, the colours looked sharper and the sun brighter. She always lifted his spirit whenever she was around.

BROOKE FINDS A SECOND HOME

Brooke was a restless soul. Even he didn't know what was gnawing at him. For some mysterious reason he could never find peace and his mind never quieted down. To help relax, as much as he possibly could, every evening Brooke would walk through Thunder Bay discovering new areas. He was the type of person that needed to know every nook and cranny. He was curious and needed to know at all times where he was. Brooke had a natural sense of direction. Rarely did he have difficulty finding his way around, even in unfamiliar areas. Nevertheless, he loved to explore and get to know every street and neighbourhood. He liked to familiarize himself with all the cafés, stores and restaurants. Nothing went unnoticed by him and quickly he knew Thunder Bay as well as, if not better than, any native.

Every time Brooke went out he took a different route, even when going to the same place. The first time he headed towards Starbucks to meet his friends, he first headed east on Andrew Street, where he lived, then turned south on Ray to the end of which he turned east onto Inchiquin street and continued till he reached Memorial and headed south to his destination. The second time he went to Starbucks he detoured west on Andrew turned south on Balmoral to Central where he turned east to Memorial, and the third time, he headed north on Frankwood from Andrew, then east on John all the way to Algoma south which then becomes Memorial. Brooke was never in a rush when heading to Starbucks, he allowed himself this leisure. At other times, when Brooke didn't have to meet anyone or work, he simply walked around discovering new and different areas.

It was still September and the weather was warm with a slight breeze. The sun was still up this early in the evening. Brooke was walking on Central Avenue, south of Oliver but west of the Thunder Bay Expressway, when a shimmer of light caught his eye. It was such a quick glimpse that he had to search the horizon for its origin. He saw it again and this time located the source. Through the trees, on the south side of Central, a window facing west off a tall building was reflecting the light of the sun. Brooke grew curious. The map had not indicated any streets beyond Vimy, where he was heading. Every time Brooke discovered a new area, he made notes on a map he had picked up at Canadian Tire. The trees were dense and it was difficult to see beyond. Brooke walked to the end of Vimy. A yellow and black 'dead end' sign stood at the edge of the asphalt. On the other side of the guardrail only trees were visible. Brooke decided to venture further in search of the building he had spotted earlier. A trail was visible off to one side through the tall grass, Brooke followed it. About thirty feet further, a different world opened up to him. Brooke had this sensation of being in a dream or an old Western movie. The scenery in front of him reminded him of a ghost town. He had read about some but never thought he would ever encounter one, especially not in this part of the world. All the ghost towns he had ever read about were located somewhere in the United States. A road long ago abandoned sat in front of him. The cracked asphalt had weeds growing through it; on each side stood old abandoned commercial buildings. Insects buzzed around quietly, a sign that not too many humans or vehicles ventured around this area. It looked as if this area had once been part of an industrial park but now it was completely abandoned and had been for several years. Nature was taking over again. Later Brooke would find out from doing some research about the place that it had been deserted some thirty years previous, following some environmental disaster. It had been very difficult to find any information about this area. The information was scarce and vague. Brooke sensed that a huge cover up had kept information out of the media. Even citizens refused to talk about it or pretended not to know anything about it. Most feigned to ignore the area ever existed. But somehow Brooke had found information confirming the area was now safe and seeing how nature had taken over, that also reassured Brooke of its safety. Why they had completely abandoned all these buildings, Brooke would never know. He assumed that was how the government wanted it to be. He had also discovered that the government owned all the land. They had seized it during the disaster. Brooke could only imagine the fortunes lost by the people running their businesses in this area.

Some of the buildings still stood complete, some boarded up, some not, others were partially demolished or had fallen apart and some only had the footing of the building left. All of them without exception had their signs removed or chiselled out, leaving them all anonymous. 'Strange', thought Brooke. The only people remaining were bums lying in boxes or in hidden corners. Shopping carts filled with other peoples' garbage were guarded by tired eyes wrapped up in tired, dirty, torn clothes. Their faces seemed to tell a story no one wanted to hear. This appeared to be where the forgotten came to finish their lives and it got Brooke thinking of how society pushes away people with problems rather than trying to help them. He couldn't help thinking of how our country seemed to love sending money away to help other countries but when it came to helping their own, they were rather prejudiced. The government wouldn't help you if you didn't have an address but you couldn't get an address if you didn't have any money. Just one of those ridiculous catch twenty-two's. Brooke couldn't help but think of this area as 'The Closet of the Forgotten', people had closed the door behind them and forgotten this section even existed, along with the bums that now populated it. From the surroundings it was obvious that police didn't patrol this area; broken syringes and alcohol bottles littered the streets. Brooke watched his step. The last thing he wanted was to catch some deadly disease but his curiosity kept him moving forward. He wondered when a cop had last set foot on these abandoned streets. It was infested with drugs Brooke could smell them as he walked by. Some of the druggies even stared straight at him while smoking whatever it was they were smoking. Their grin put Brooke on the defence. He pulled his hood over his head and tried to blend in. He concealed his face that was a little too clean when compared to the people from this area but he couldn't do much about the clothes. Although his mind wandered, his eyes registered everything around him. He tried not to notice the rats and mice crawling in the grungy corners and he avoided eye contact with the loafers. Although he felt sorry for them, they still made him feel uncomfortable.

Suddenly a large boarded building caught his attention. This structure looked like it once had been an important warehouse. It was sandwiched between two other buildings almost the same size, now all standing together abandoned. The buildings on each side were crumbling but this particular building was still complete and almost seemed to be calling his name. Brooke had a strange sense of calm and belonging at the sight of the building.

Curiosity sharpened, his eyes scanned for any possible openings. He casually walked around the whole building discreetly looking for an opening. It was in an alleyway behind the building, that Brooke finally found an opening through a broken window hidden behind a long forgotten dumpster. He squeezed his slender body through the narrow opening, careful of not leaning against the ragged edges of glass around the frame and made his way inside without anyone noticing.

Once inside, his eyes adjusted to the darkness within a few seconds. Enough street light made its' way in, allowing Brooke to get a basic idea of the layout. In the centre of the warehouse a wide wooden staircase with a wrought iron handrail led the way to an upper floor. After scanning the first floor for potential dangers or occupants, Brooke cautiously made his way up. On the second floor the window barricades weren't as heavy, thus allowing slightly more light to penetrate. Brooke stood at the top of the stairs staring along the double width hallway which led to two single French doors on each side and a set of double French doors straight ahead. The floors were thin strip hard wood, yellow with old varnish. Cobwebs occupied every corner, doorway and crevice.

From the layout of the second floor Brooke understood this had been the office area. A few pieces of furniture had been abandoned. Despite the heavy dust and cobwebs this space had an immediate calming effect on Brooke. He decided that very moment this would be his sanctuary. He intended on spending a lot of time here despite having to walk through the bum and drug infested streets.

Slowly Brooke made his way around absorbing these new surroundings. He wanted to check out each office when he heard a weak meow. He searched around following the sound of the meowing. It sounded like there was more than one cat or kitten. Finally, in a corner underneath a chair he saw a mother with two little kittens. The mother was so skinny and looked weak from nursing her little ones. The cat hissed at Brooke. Patiently, he reassured it by walking slowly bent forward with his arm stretched forward and gently talking to it. The mother settled after sniffing Brooke's hand for a few minutes. The mother had long, charcoal grey fur and emerald green eyes. The kittens were no bigger than a mouse. Brooke knew that they could not be more than a week old. One's fur was identical to the mother, charcoal grey and the other was all grey except for the tip of its paws and tail which were white. Both had blue eyes but Brooke knew that would change in a few months.

Brooke found an old plant saucer, poured water from his bottle, and put it close to the mother's head. Then he took a banana from his pocket, he always had a snack in his pockets because he sometimes forgot to eat and then hunger would suddenly strike violently. He put a small piece of the banana next to the bowl. He had no idea if she would eat it but she looked so skinny. The mother slowly got up pulling away from her kittens. She smelled the banana and quickly devoured it. Brooke was surprised to see her eat it, then turn around and meow for more. He gave her more until she stopped eating and lay back with her little ones.

After taking care of the cats, Brooke inspected the rest of the abandoned warehouse and made a mental note of the things he would need to clean up the place a little. After a few hours Brooke left once again following a new route home. He followed one of the abandoned roads heading east. All the street names in this deserted area had been removed. He had never seen or heard of anything like this. Anything and everything that could relay any information about this place had been eliminated, destroyed or removed. This road led him under the Thunder Bay Expressway. He continued further into a small forest where the trees were still fairly young. Passed this forest he ended up in the back of a building housed in the current industrial area. This building faced Innovation Drive. From there Brooke walked north to Central Avenue, then east to Balmoral. He walked north on Balmoral all the way to Andrew street. By the time he got home it was two o'clock in the morning, the whole town was quiet. Just the way he liked it.

The next day Brooke went back bringing with him a broom, dustpan, rags, and some garbage bags. He had stuffed all these items, except for the broomstick, in a backpack. In a large bag he had a basket for the cats, some cat food and some bowls he had purchased on his way to his new and secret hideaway. The first thing he did was feed the mother and then he set the basket close to her litter. He knew he shouldn't touch the kittens until the mother fully trusted him. The mother devoured the food and drank some water. Then she proceeded to moving her two kittens into the basket before settling in with them. Brooke watched discretely from a distance. He didn't want to scare the mother away. He feared that if he made the cat uncomfortable she would remove her little ones to a different location and then he might not be able to care for them. He always had a soft spot for cats, especially kittens.

The cats settled he turned to the real reason he was there. Brooke intended to clean the place up a little, make it more pleasant. The warehouse was quite a large two-story building with high ceilings. The warehouse ceiling, Brooke estimated, to be approximately twenty-two feet high and the offices he thought were about twelve feet high. These high ceilings gave the place a sense of grandeur which really appealed to Brooke. It took away any sensation of claustrophobia and seemed to provide a protective shield against the world outside. From the appliqués on the ceiling, Brooke guessed the building might have been built in the late nineteenth century or early twentieth, when workers built with pride.

As Brooke swept he also looked around imagining what it might have looked like originally. A few pieces of furniture had been left over from the hay days of the late business it once housed. Brooke got busy dusting and cleaning as good as he possibly could with the accessories he had. He also made notes of other things he wanted to bring with him next time.

By the time he left he had filled three garbage bags and had not even gotten a quarter of the second floor cleaned up. It would take him at least a couple of weeks to get it all done but he welcomed the project. Brooke was not one to stay idle.

From that moment on, every moment Brooke could spare he went to the warehouse and worked on cleaning it up. He had added a battery-operated lamp to the belongings he kept at the warehouse. Certain parts of the place didn't allow much streetlight to penetrate. Somehow the streetlights still worked in this area. Brooke assumed they forgot about them, yet they had been so careful to get rid of all the signs, or it was too costly to sever the underground connection. He suspected the latter to be the most likely.

The room he had found most interesting was the president's office. At least he assumed it had been the president's. It was the largest room on the floor and was occupied by a very large and expensive looking desk made of hard wood - he wasn't sure what kind of wood exactly - decorated with ornate carvings, a large leather chair with a mahogany frame sat slightly askew from the desk. Every wall was laid-out with floor to ceiling built-in mahogany bookcases which only contained a handful of dusty, yellow-paged books but Brooke could easily imagine how impressive it must have been when it had been filled with books. This became his favourite room. The ladder that had once served to reach the top shelves lay broken on the floor. Brooke carefully inspected it. He hoped he might be able to restore it. To do so, he knew he would need some carpenters' glue, some grips, and a few other tools.

Every time Brooke left the warehouse, he felt good about his accomplishments. It gave him a sense of pride. He particularly enjoyed the fact that he didn't share the place with anyone. It was his and his alone.

He was always very cautious whenever he entered or exited the place. He didn't want to attract attention to his hideaway. He planned on making a door to fit the window so he may lock the place up to protect it from being discovered or used by anyone else.

After a few weeks of Brooke coming to the warehouse almost every day the cat began greeting him at the top of the stairs. She would meow her welcome to him and rub herself against his legs as he tried to walk towards the basket. He had given each one a name; the mother was Mistress, the one that was completely grey, like it's mother, was Smokey, and the other kitten with the white paws he called it Butler, because it looked like it had gloves on. The kittens grew quickly and soon started eating on their own.

THE SEARCH CONTINUES

It was late October and Christa Makins had been missing for four months now. Rebecca Reese was worried sick about her niece. She knew Christa didn't have an easy life and wished she could help her ease the pain and lead her towards a better and easier future. Rebecca wanted to give Christa the type of life she would have given her own children, had she ever became a mother herself. It was hard for Rebecca to sit by and let her sister treat a child the same way they had been treated as children, which was the main reason Rebecca hadn't spoken to her since Christa was a baby. It tore Rebecca's heart knowing she couldn't do anything about it. She preferred not to stand by and watch. After the phone call on that fatal day in June, Rebecca Reese inquired whether her sister, Sara, and husband, Hank Makins, had any other children, and was relieved to find they had not created more victims. She had Higgleton, a private investigator, check all the birth records of Echo Bay and surrounding towns.

She also suspected that Christa, most likely, did not miss her parents. No kid could ever miss parents like these, drinking all the time, yelling and screaming for no reason. Rebecca knew the scene all too well. Her parents had been the same way, but she had decided to make a better life for herself and succeeded. She had left the day of her eighteenth birthday. She had planned her departure since she was about eight years old. The night before her birthday, she packed all her belongings before she went to bed, but she couldn't sleep at all that night. The morning of her birthday, she had gotten up before everyone else and simply left, leaving a goodbye letter taped to the refrigerator door. She had later communicated with her sister hoping to persuade her to follow, but it was too late. Sara was already pregnant and planning to marry Hank Makins. Their communications after that had been very scarce and mostly argumentative, until one day they stopped talking altogether. Rebecca disagreed with the path her sister had chosen, but was never able to persuade her to do any differently.

Rebecca had to work very hard to achieve her goals. But she was determined to show them all what she was made of. What she learned through the process is that her family really didn't care. In the end she really did it to prove to herself that she wasn't like them, and that she could achieve whatever it was that she wanted. And she had done that very well. She ran her own business, called Agent Reese & Soldiers, which employed a dozen people.

She had created her waterfront dream home, in the penthouse of a Chicago high-rise with a panoramic view of Lake Michigan. Her penthouse was a forty seven hundred square foot two bedroom condo with floor to ceiling windows facing the lake. The kitchen, family room, library, dining room, and living room formed a glassed half circle at the back of the unit, facing the waterfront. Opposite that circle was a study which led to the master bedroom, and parallel to it was a spare bedroom. Each room had double glass doors leading to a balcony. The decor was very contemporary with streamlined furniture. It was like walking into a European decor magazine. The half circle room was an open concept harmoniously divided into spaces with different purposes. As you walked out of the private elevator a large hall closet stood on the left. Straight ahead was the main living area. The bedrooms were cleverly accessible, but out of direct sight. Both bedrooms were complete with Ensuites, outfitted with all the features you would find at a spa, such as an air bath with chromatherapy, baskets with essential oils, and sea salts were conveniently displayed. Built-in speakers were integrated throughout the whole condo with the individual controls in each bedroom and Ensuite. The music could be played in every room at once, or each room could select something different. The rooms were sound proof, avoiding the sounds from each room overlapping one another.

Rebecca had a maid come in twice a week when she was not traveling. If she was abroad then the cleaning service came only once a week. She ate out most nights with clients, and employees. Agent Reese & Soldiers was the most important sales agency in Chicago. She had started this business six years ago as a one-woman show from the small apartment she was renting at the time, and had slowly grown the business by hiring one representative at a time, and training them personally. She had quickly developed a favourable reputation, and was continuously pursued by manufacturers. The retailers she dealt with had become close relations, and were always eager to see new lines she brought to the market. Within four months of business she had had no choice but to hire help, and from then she had hired two new representatives each year. Rebecca took the time to show them the ropes, and training them to her own personal requirements. She knew her customers, and knew what they expected, and therefore trained her staff accordingly.

She held sales meetings monthly. This allowed Rebecca to keep everyone up-to-date on new information or lines. During these meetings she provided training sessions, and open discussions. Everybody worked as a team. Rebecca did not tolerate bickering or internal competition. She treated them like family, and expected them to treat each other the same way.

Since the month of June, Rebecca had been putting off hiring another sales rep because she wanted to be able to give Christa her full attention - when she finally found her - but Rebecca would soon have to cave in. Business was growing so fast that she might have to consider hiring more than one representative this time. She had even considered starting her own sales school, of course she would keep it as part of the internal business. This option might make the recruiting a little easier, and keep recruiting to once a year rather than twice, enabling her to train several representatives at once.

Christa's mother, Sara, on the other hand just fell right into her parents' footsteps. Rebecca had tried several times to convince her sister to let her raise the baby. She wanted to save Christa the pain, and abuse of alcoholic parents. She remembered the conversations well; "What makes you think you can raise a baby?" Christa's mother would say, "You can't even keep a man." These words cut like a knife. She had never told Christa's mother that their father had robbed her of any hope of building a family or having a normal life. She knew Sara had escaped their fathers' grip. They were so close in age, by the time Rebecca left home, Sara left shortly after. She married Hank at the young age of sixteen. Looking for the love she never felt in her family, simply to end up in the same trap.

Like many young women from a dysfunctional family, Sara had held on to the first guy that paid attention to her, looking for love in all the wrong places, thinking that if you have sex with a guy he'll automatically love you back. Within months Sara was pregnant, which led to her premature wedding.

Rebecca had moved to the States when she left home. She felt like she couldn't get far enough from her parents. At first, Rebecca had stayed in contact with her sister, but they never did see eye to eye, and Rebecca was the only one making an effort. Sara thought the world of Hank, and listened only to him. Their parents were all too happy to be rid of them, and encouraged the situation. The sisters completely stopped talking to each other before Christa was even a year old. Unfortunately, this prevented Rebecca Reese from ever knowing her niece. Christa didn't even know that Rebecca existed. The sisters had not spoken for over sixteen years.

That critical day in June when Christa ran away, and her parents perished in the fire, Rebecca hired a private investigator, Mr. Higgleton, to locate her missing niece. Now, four months later, they still had no clue where she was. Not knowing her niece didn't help. She couldn't get into her mind to guess where she could have headed. Rebecca had no idea if Christa had any friends, and if so who they might be. She didn't know what dreams drove her niece, what she wanted from life or herself. Rebecca was clueless.

The private investigator Rebecca hired was an ex-RCMP (Royal Canadian Mounted Police) officer. She trusted that he would know the area and the people well, since Mr. Higgleton had been born, raised, and still lived in Homepayne, which wasn't too far from Echo Bay. Higgleton had lived many places across the country during his career with the RCMP, but returned home as soon as the RCMP allowed him to go back. He preferred the northern forests of Ontario. Rebecca had interviewed five investigators that day. Mr. Higgleton seamed genuine, and eager to help for the right reasons. This didn't seem to be just a job for him.

Higgleton was a tall man with silver hair. His features gave away his multi-cultural roots. The aboriginal blood in him seemed to attract him to the deep woods of the area. He was of Ojibwa descent from the area of Sault Ste. Marie on his mother's side, and inherited his English name, and blood from his great-great-grand father. Higgleton

30

had a square jaw that gave him authority, but his dark brown eyes were kind. He was very tall, and built from strong large bones. Although his height was impressive he looked pretty harmless. His years of training, and working with the RCMP made him dangerous to the enemy. His instincts were strong, and he trusted them without hesitation. Higgleton had a kind heart, and despised people that took advantage of others.

The search was very difficult. No pictures of Christa were ever located. If there ever had been any they had burned in the house fire. He had to depend on the description he got from the grocer of her. The grocer and his wife were of the few people who knew the girl. The girl seemed almost inexistent. The local high school in Sault Ste. Marie had no record of her, but the librarian and some students seemed to know her from the description given by the grocery store owners, but nobody knew her name. Even that lead was shaky at best. The people that recognized her description had seen her in the library every morning from eight thirty to about ten thirty every morning during most of the school year. The local motel also had a maid that fit the description, but knew her only as Sophie; she had worked from eleven in the morning to about two in the afternoon. The school bus driver knew the girl described to him, and confirmed taking her to and from the high school every day. He even showed Higgleton the pick-up, and drop-off location, which was on the main road a few hundred feet from the dirt road leading to the Makins house. Everything fit together, but led nowhere. No one had seen her since the end of June, but they all assumed it was because the school year had ended. The motel owner was the only one who thought something was odd because the two previous summers Christa had worked. She had never mentioned to him anything about quitting or leaving. He would have called police, but he didn't have much information to give them. All he ever had on her was a first name, Sophie. He had never asked for an address or anything else. He knew she would never give him the real one, so what was the point. He had seen many girls like her come and go. He never refused them work. He knew somehow he was helping them by allowing them to make some money of their own, and always hoped they would use it to better their situations, get away from the abusers in their lives.

Higgleton was a good tracker, but Christa had covered her trail well. He sensed that Christa had planned her escape very carefully, and over a very long period of time. When he shared this information with Rebecca Reese, she recognized some of her own character traits in the girl, and longed even more to find her quickly. She felt that Christa and her shared much of the same genes. Although she had not known Christa, deep down, she always felt like Christa should have been her child.

The pieces to the puzzle seem to fit together indicating that this schedule belonged to Christa, but it ended there. Higgleton had inspected the burnt house for further clues, and had found the trail leading to a cave. There he found discarded clothing, and further up the trail he observed car tracks leaving the woods. They had confirmed Christa's DNA from the clothing found in the cave by comparing it to her parents. This confirmed Christa's escape, and it also put her in the system so that if anything came up, they could easily identify her. Although everything indicated Christa premeditated her escape, the police still ruled the fire accidental, the fire department hadn't found anything to suggest otherwise.

With very little to go on, Higgleton continued his search in Sault Ste. Marie but found nothing more. He extended his search to surrounding towns, but they were all very small towns surrounded with acres of forest. It was so easy for someone to disappear, never to be found. The car tracks from the trail had revealed the make of the car, but there were none registered under the Makins name, another dead end.

There were many cars of that make and model in the area, too many to research individually. Higgleton looked up all ownership transfers dated within the six months preceding Christa's disappearance. Nothing pointed in Christa's direction.

BROOKE TALKS TO HIMSELF

Gregory was walking towards Starbucks to meet his friends. It was a grey day, nothing particular about the weather. This time of year the weather was usually grey in Thunder Bay. Warm, sunny days became rare and you didn't exactly know when the snow would hit until you could smell it in the fresh, cold air. As Greg walked through the park he noticed Brooke ahead. His pace grew suddenly faster to catch up to him but then he slowed down again when he noticed that Brooke seemed to be in a very animated conversation. He approached cautiously as he was looking to see whom Brooke was talking with. No matter where Greg looked, he saw no one. Gregory grew more puzzled the closer he got. He could now hear Brookes' conversation.

"I'm so fed up! I'm fed up of playing these games. I can't even be myself. Never could. First it was because of the parents, now it's because of the world. Am I ever going to be able to just live the way I want?" Brooke's arms were swinging around in exasperation. His face was contorted into several different expressions of frustration. He continued this way for a few minutes longer, and then suddenly he stopped and sat on a bench leaning forward his face in his hands. He remained immobile for a while. During that time, Gregory stayed out of sight trying to understand what was going on, he still could not see anyone else anywhere and he never heard any one respond to Brooke.

After a few minutes Gregory saw Brooke look up again. His face seemed completely changed, almost serene. Brooke slowly stood up and started walking towards Starbucks, as if nothing had happened. Perplexed, Gregory followed from a distance at first still looking for whom ever Brooke had been speaking to. Finally he caught up to Brooke. He had never met Brooke's brother, Dale, and had no idea what their relationship was like. Brooke never talked about it.

"Hey Man! What's up?" Brooke said first, looking and sounding his usual self.

"Hey! Not much, how about you?" Gregory thought it wasn't wise to mention what he had witnessed just now, but just couldn't ignore it.

"You know. The usual," Brooke continued. "Are you coming to the Voo-Doo Lounge later tonight?"

"Hey what was that all about back there?" Greg decided to confront Brooke about it.

"What?"

"Who were you talking to?"

"Eh! No one," Brooke looked embarrassed. "I… I was talking to myself."

"To yourself?" Greg grew even more confused.

"That was nothing. I was just practicing a part." Brooke looked straight ahead, avoiding Greg.

"Bud! I'm a little confused here. Acting part?" Gregory had stopped walking and was staring directly at Brooke who was looking at the ground.

"I'm trying out for a local play." Brooke still wouldn't look at Greg. He was beyond embarrassed now. "Please don't tell the others. They'll tear me apart over this, and you know it."

"Okay," Gregory agreed. He didn't want to embarrass his friend any more then he already was. "What is it about?"

"Can we drop it and talk about something else?" Brooke didn't wait for Greg's response. "So, are you coming to the Lounge tonight?"

"Yeah! Why?" Gregory responded mechanically.

"There's someone I want you to meet." Brooke had a conspiring smile on his face.

"Who?" Gregory hated surprise introductions.

"Ah! It's a surprise." Brooke's sly smile grew even larger. They argued about it for a few minutes, but Brooke never gave in. Brooke never took no for an answer.

That evening, Greg walked into the Voo-Doo Lounge later than usual. He was dreading the surprise intro. He headed straight to the bar where Brooke was talking with a few girls as he served their drinks. Greg could tell that Brooke came equipped with his usual charm. The girls were laughing, and looking at Brooke in very flirtatious manners.

He knew how to work them. Odd for someone who never went out with the girls. Gregory wondered where Brooke had learned how to handle women like that. Usually, the players had a way with the women, but Brooke wasn't a player, he was an avoider.

Greg sat on his usual stool at the end of the bar, and waited for Brooke to notice his presence. He looked around to see who was around. The crowd usually consisted of the same people night after night. The odd night you would see an unfamiliar face. Greg felt kind of moody. He didn't like when Brooke introduced him to new people. He always used the job as an excuse not to be rude to the ladies, but Greg hated being the scapegoat.

"Hey Bud! What took you so long?" Startled Greg spun around to face Brooke. Brooke settled a bottle of Rickard's Red in front of him. Greg's preferred drink.

"Just had a few things to do," offered Greg. "The place is pretty busy tonight, maybe I shouldn't stick around."

"What do you mean? No! You should stay and have some fun." Brooke didn't want Greg to leave. He enjoyed Greg's company when he was at work. "Besides, you haven't met Carolynn yet." Greg made a face as Brooke added that last part.

"Is that another one of those girls you're just gonna pawn off on me?" Greg said. He was dreading the intro.

"I don't just pawn girls off on you. I thought you liked meeting girls," Brooke felt panicky. He really didn't want to be left alone to deal with this girl. Carolynn had been bugging Brooke for the past week. Brooke kept acting uninterested, but that didn't seem to dissuade her in the least. Actually, it seemed to have the reverse effect. She was persistent. Greg wondered why Brooke never pursued any of the girls. He could pretty much have his pick. They basically threw themselves at him.

People at the other end of the bar were waiting, so Brooke just left Greg to serve his other customers. A few minutes later he came back to Greg's end of the bar.

"So, is this another one of those clingy chicks?" Greg said as Brooke leaned against the bar in front of him.

"But you're so good at giving them the message. I can't risk losing customers. You know that." That same old excuse again. Greg was tired of hearing it.

"So, you do want me to do your dirty work, once again…" Greg sighed. "I'll do it this one last time, but next time you're on your own. No! Actually next time I'll just start a rumour that you are gay. Yeah! Wouldn't that be fun?"

"Ah! Come on man! I thought we were a team." Brooke tried to coax Greg. Greg stared back with a look that said he was dead serious. He didn't understand Brooke, and what he had witnessed earlier really disturbed him. He didn't believe Brooke's acting story. He wondered if his friend had mental issues. That scene perturbed him. He wasn't quite sure why, but it just did.

"Greg!" Brooke called out to him as a tall blond approached the bar. "This is Carolynn. Carolynn, this is Greg," he introduced the two then excused himself. Customers were waiting at the other end of the bar again.

"Hi!" Carolynn smiled, "So you're the famous Greg. Brooke told me so much about you." Her voice was almost a purr and Greg had to admit she was drop dead gorgeous. Why the hell wouldn't Brooke want to go out with this one? He decided he would still give her a run for her money.

"Oh! Yeah? Tell me what he said, and I'll tell you if any of it is true," Greg said a smug look on his face.

"Well, the first thing he said was that you would look annoyed at first. He said you don't really like meeting new people." She laughed as she said this. Gregory couldn't quite make out the colour of her eyes in this lighting but he could tell they were a rare shade of blue or green. The blonde hair looked natural, and her skin bore a tanned glow. Gregory also noticed that Carolynn had a toned body from working out. This girl took good care of herself. That was a trait Greg highly admired.

Greg was startled at first by Carolynn's frankness, but then was seduced by her sense of humour. Within minutes the two were huddled together to better hear one another through the loud music, and hundreds of conversations around them. Greg laughed harder than he had ever remembered laughing. By the end of the evening his face and stomach were sore. Several hours had gone by when Carolynn started squinting at her watch.

"Holy! Is it really two am?" She stared at Greg eyes wide with surprise.

"You bet ch'ya." Brooke answered with a mischievous grin on his face, "You two having too much fun?"

Greg's face went flush, and he gave Brooke a dirty look. Brooke simply raised both hands and shoulders, and turned around. He went to look after other customers.

Greg and Carolynn planned to meet again the next night. This time Greg was glad that Brooke had introduced him. He just wasn't ready to admit it yet. Carolynn was nothing like he had imagined. She was not only beautiful, but smart as well. She worked as a secretary, and took correspondence courses in Marketing. She had been born and raised in Thunder Bay. She had never been interested in Brooke. Greg was the one she wanted to meet, and had simply gone after Brooke because she knew he always pawned the girls off onto Gregory. She had watched him do it several times over the last few months. This was a sure way of getting Greg's attention.

Gregory often stayed after the bar closed while Brooke cleaned up, and balanced his cash. They talked very little. Within forty minutes, Brooke was done, and ready to go. When Brooke first started, it would take him an hour and half to close up his bar, but now he knew the drill, and was usually out within forty-five minutes. Rarely did his cash not balance, that fact usually determined how long it would take. If he didn't balance, then he would have to count the money over again, and double-check everything. Brooke put his tips in his pocket, put on his jacket, and walked outside accompanied by Greg. A few blocks away they parted ways, and Brooke went straight home.

SATURDAY WITH GENEVA

Geneva knocked on Dale's door at precisely eight o'clock. She was always punctual. Today was the big Saturday. Dale couldn't wait to see everything she had planned for them. Although she had run the schedule by him during the week, he was sure she probably added a few surprises. First they were going out for breakfast. Geneva had pointed out the fact that they would need a lot of energy to walk around, and see all the attractions. They were lucky it was a beautiful sunny, and warm, fall day. The sun brought out all the beautiful colours from the trees and landscape.

They drove to Dimitri's, located on South Court Street, for breakfast. There Geneva refreshed Dale's memory regarding the day's schedule.

After he finished his eggs Florentine, and Geneva had eaten her fruit and cottage cheese, they headed to the Fort William Historical Park. Dale drove down Memorial Avenue then took the Harbour Expressway to Highway 17, on to Highway 61 then got off on Broadway Avenue from which they reached King Road to the park. It was a fairly short drive, but too far to walk.

A costumed tour guide led the way into the Fort. Entering the citadel left a lasting impression. No words could truly describe the experience, but it was like stepping onto the scene of an old cowboy and Indian movie. Everything was frozen in time. So many people walked about their business as if the modern world did not exist. All the costumes looked authentic, and no modern machinery or buildings existed beyond the entrance gate. It was quite spectacular. Then Dale caught Geneva, from the corner of his eye, staring at him. Taking in his expressions and reaction to the sight, at that very moment Dale felt the blood rush up his face. He thought his face went purple that time. He was beyond the red and crimson colour phase. He tried to act normal, although he knew she had already seen the embarrassment in his face. She simply smiled back, and they proceeded to following their guide.

"I'm really glad we don't live this way anymore," Dale commented. Everyone seemed to work so hard. He could not imagine himself having to work so hard physically.

"Me too!" was Geneva's response. "I would really miss the daily showers." With that comment they both burst laughing.

It was really interesting to see how everything was handcrafted. They didn't have any machines to help them, and if they needed to communicate the only way was person to person, or via letter. Most impressive of all is how much they could accomplish with so little. They really had to be creative. A flash from the past gave Dale a jolt. Suddenly he was having difficulty breathing, and had to stop. Geneva looked at him.

"Are you okay?" Her concern showed all over her face as she reached for his arms. He raised his right hand to stop her from grabbing him.

"I'm fine," he answered. "Just a little asthma," he lied. Dale didn't want Geneva knowing about his anxiety attacks. He knew if she found out she would ask too many questions. Questions he did not want to answer.

They continued their tour at a leisurely pace. The tour took almost two hours. From there they made their way to the Thunder Bay Museum on Donald Street. The building looked like a grade or junior high school, but in fact used to be a police station and courthouse. It got Dale wondering about how government decided facility locations. Who decided where the police station, city hall, library, post office, and so on would be located. And why would they ever want to move these important public services? These things boggled his mind.

"Dale?" Geneva broke Dale's reverie.

"Yeah?"

"Did you see this?" She was pointing at an old document dated from the early nineteenth century.

"It's when you see all these few hundred year old documents, tools, furniture, and what-ever else these things are, that you realize that it's all a big wheel that keeps turning." This comment just blurted out of Dale without realizing he had spoken out loud. Geneva simply smiled at him, he knew she understood what he meant, and they continued fascinated by all that surrounded them. Dale realized even more then how similar their personalities were. Geneva and Dale shared a lot of the same interests. It felt nice to finally meet someone that could understand him.

They spent a few hours at the museum admiring all the items so amazingly well preserved for so many years.

"I hope you are hungry because I am starving," Geneva said as they walked out of the museum. She was squinting against the blinding light of the sun. The museum lights were no match to the sun.

"I could eat a horse," Dale responded, and they ran to the car. They were still giggling as they drove off. "Where to, Missy?"

Geneva directed him to the Hoito Restaurant in the Finnish district. As they walked into this café style restaurant, his mouth started watering. It smelled so delicious.

"This place was established in 1918," Geneva told Dale. "At first, it was mainly for the Finnish bush workers, but has become a landmark, here in Thunder Bay. You cannot, and I mean can not, visit Thunder Bay without eating here at least once." She ended with a grin, "That's what I read in the tourism guide."

"Well, it sure smells amazing, and since you are in charge of my social education, I will let you order my dinner." Geneva looked at him, and he could tell that she already knew what to order. Lost in their fascination with all the sites, they had skipped lunch. At this point Dale was so hungry he could have eaten anything.

"Are you sure you trust me for this? It's my first time here too."

Geneva and Dale were having pleasant conversation when Dale suddenly felt eyes upon him. He looked around to see who was staring. That is when he noticed a man looking down on him as if he thought he was better than Dale. Dale brought this to Geneva's attention, and said; "Look at the way he's looking at us. How can he judge us without even knowing us?"

"Just let it go," Geneva said resting a hand on his. "You shouldn't worry about what other people think." But Dale kept feeling this guy's eyes burning a hole in him.

He started getting uncomfortable, and began to be eager to get out of the restaurant. But Geneva was still eating, and he didn't feel like he had any right rushing her. She kept telling Dale not to worry about it. "The guy probably had a bad day. Maybe it's not even us he's staring at," she insisted. Geneva tried to convince him that the guy was probably in a blank stare. Dale couldn't be happier when they finally walked out.

When Dale finally got home it was past eight o'clock. It had been a long, fun day. Brooke had to go out, but couldn't come out until Dale was home. Dale said good night to Geneva, thanked her for a wonderful day, and went inside.

An hour later, Brooke walked out of the house dressed in black slacks and dress shoes, black turtleneck, and leather jacket. His hair was spiked, and he walked with the confidence of someone who knew where he belonged in life. Brooke looked more like a city boy than anyone in Thunder Bay. He was an outcast in his own way. Whether that was good or bad still remained to be seen, but his popularity seemed to indicate that it was good. Brooke headed straight to work. There wasn't enough time to kill with his friends, besides he would see them at the Lounge later.

PARANOIA SETS IN

"What?" Brooke snapped at his friends as he walked into Starbuck's. He didn't like when they stared at him like that. It made him feel nervous, "Why are you all looking at me that way?"

"What are you talking about?" Gregory spoke up as he turned to look at Brooke entering.

"I saw everyone staring at me. Why were you all looking at me that way?" Brooke felt very defensive.

"We weren't looking at you until you barked at us." Gregory had noticed Brooke's paranoia before. He was starting to suspect something wasn't quite right with his friend. Especially since he had caught him talking to himself, he had tried to approach the subject, but Brooke insisted that he had been practicing for a play. He knew Brooke didn't take drugs, nor drank much, so he couldn't blame it on substance influence. Something wasn't right. Greg would have liked to know what it was, so he could understand Brooke's outbursts better and probably help avoid or, at least, subside them. Brooke snapped more and more often for no apparent reason. Greg was worried, and the others annoyed.

"Brooke, don't be like that. No one was staring. Just calm down, man!" Gregory was the only one that could talk reason with Brooke. Brooke sat down looking bewildered. He looked like a trapped animal. Gregory got him his usual latté, and set it in front of him. Hoping this would soothe him a little.

"I'm worried about you," attempted Gregory. "You're getting a little too paranoid. What's bothering you, man?" Gregory knew prying wouldn't get him very far, but he still had to try.

"Nothing! What makes you think something's wrong?" Brooke wasn't fooling any one, "I'm just tired, that's all." He turned to look out the window. Gregory knew Brooke well enough that when Brooke said he was tired it really meant that something was bothering him, but good luck getting it out of him. He had tried many times in the last few months.

"So, what's the verdict?" Brooke always got very anxious when he felt under pressure to talk. He quickly changed the subject. "Where are we going?"

"You know what, man? I think I'm just gonna head home," Peter was the first to speak up.

"Why," Brooke asked.

"I got stuff to do," was all Peter would offer for an answer as he got up and left.

"Yeah! Me too," Josh followed. "Hey Pete wait up!"

"What's with them?" Brooke turned towards Gregory, acting as if he had nothing to do with their friends' sudden departure.

"Why ask me? You should ask them." Gregory didn't want to get in the middle of it. Although he knew that the guys didn't like being around Brooke when he was in this mood. He didn't want to be the one to tell him.

"Let's go see a movie then," Brooke suggested.

Gregory didn't want to contradict Brooke further. He simply started suggesting a few titles.

After the movie, Brooke walked home alone, but he didn't go directly home. He decided to stop at his secret hideaway for a moment of peace. For some weird reason this place was where he felt most comfortable. His mind felt at peace when he was there. It was as if nothing else existed. He was in his perfect little world. So he slipped behind the usual garbage bin, through the broken window, into the abandoned warehouse. Having grown up in the woods, the city life required much adjustment for Brooke. He was not used to the hustle and bustle. Although Thunder Bay is not a huge city, it still was a big change from the quiet forest.

The warehouse had once entertained offices on the upper level. Brooke ran up the stairs, and sat on a windowsill at the front of the building. He peeked through a crack in the board covering the window. The usual bums roamed the abandoned streets. It was like watching one of those sci-fi movies about the future. Then he started to wonder if the future really was going to be so grim. No. He refused to believe it. What would be the point of going on if it were the case?

Some of the office walls had been torn down, giving a better view of the whole place. Brooke liked to imagine how he could turn the place into a loft. He visualized the brick walls exposed on each side where other buildings joined. These walls wouldn't let the heat escape. In his imaginary loft Brooke planned a laboratory kitchen on the right of the staircase. On the left he envisioned the living room slash bedroom area where a very contemporary Murphy bed and shelving unit surrounded with low profile leather couches. He could see it clear as day. Every time he came, new elements added themselves to his dream loft. One thing that never changed was his determination to, one day, have a place like this that he could call his own. He held on to this dream as if it were a life jacket. It kept his hopes up, and gave him the strength to work hard towards a better life. It helped him through the rough patches.

After about an hour he felt calm enough to go home. That night he only meditated while petting Mistress, the cat. Mistress always came to sit on his lap when he sat on the window ledge. It was their thing. Their quiet time.

The next day Brooke didn't feel like dealing with his friends, and it was a night off work, so he headed directly for the warehouse. The night before he had come to a decision, this warehouse had obviously been abandoned for a while. Brooke had not noticed any signs of recent presence in the building. As far as he could tell, nobody ever went there to check on anything. Today he was going to start working on his fantasy loft, he would strip the second floor of its' remaining walls.

Brooke felt so excited he couldn't wait to get started. He was wearing his oldest jeans and a shirt he didn't care much for anymore. He had even bought a few basic tools that he would keep at the warehouse. He already knew where he could store them during his absence.

Weeks went by, Brooke went to work as usual, but then he would head straight to the warehouse, and work on his project. On his nights off, he went directly to the warehouse, and spent all his evenings working on this project. Although, it was mostly fantasy in a way, he knew he could never finish the place the way he imagined. There would never be any furniture added to the place, and it was impossible to get electricity and running water. It still made him feel good to do as much as he could. It was something to do, and somewhere to go.

Gregory came by the Lounge a few times while he worked to see what was up. To his dismay, Brooke would just blow him off. He didn't have any interest in going to waste time with them anymore. They never did anything interesting, and Brooke just couldn't be bothered. After that last fight he completely lost interest in his friends, if he could call them that.

The second floor of the warehouse was really shaping up. Brooke would soon be ready to start rebuilding according to his plans. He made sure to salvage everything he could reuse for that purpose. He knew he wouldn't be able to bring new materials into the place without drawing attention. This cautious procedure delayed him most during destruction. He was also very careful about making sure he wasn't being watched when entering, or exiting the premises. He could never be too careful.

Brooke planned to forage other buildings for the missing materials he would require once he used up everything he already had. That might not even be necessary, as he intended to put up fewer walls than he had tore down. He wouldn't touch the main office, his favourite room. That would be the library. The solid wood bookshelves were too precious to destroy, and he loved that room. He managed to clean the room nicely. It had taken him a whole week to polish the bookcases, and repair the ladder. It was all worth it. Seeing that room always gave him the courage to continue.

At the end of every night, he swept all the litter to the ground floor, and then in a corner. He couldn't take it outside to the bin; the risks of drawing attention to himself and to the building were too great.

OUCH!!!

Brooke walked into Starbucks smiling from ear to ear. He had started hanging out with his friends again. After several weeks, Greg had finally convinced him to come back. He thought everything was going well, but that day his misconception was rectified, a far cry from what he expected.

"Hey guys! What's up?" He walked with a bounce to the usual corner table. His friends were already waiting, as the routine had always been, but they didn't seem happy to see him.

"What's with the long faces," he asked.

"Brooke, we're tired of always hanging around here waiting for you." Josh risked. They all hated confronting him, but enough was enough. Brooke had started hanging out with the guys again once he got out of his mood, and with much persuasiveness from Greg. Greg had faithfully gone to the Lounge, and with much persistence had finally convinced Brooke to hang out again. Brooke's punctuality, when it came to meeting his friends, had not improved, and the guys resented him for it.

"Yeah, we don't like the way you treat us. You act as if you think you're better than us, or something." Peter backed his friend. Everyone nodded as he spoke. Greg stared at Brooke. His expression said; 'they have a point'.

"Tomorrow, if you are not here on time you won't find any of us waiting." Josh spoke again, feeling courageous. The room filled with a dead silence. Everyone had a mournful expression.

"You know what? I don't need you guys. I can hang out with anyone I choose. You guys want to be like this I'm out of here." Brooke turned on his heels, and left the coffee house faster than he had entered. No one tried to stop him.

"I don't need these losers," he mumbled to himself as he leaped onto the sidewalk. He walked back towards his house, walked right by it. Brooke felt too wired to go home yet. He headed for the park, and sat on a bench for a while. Tonight was his night off work; he didn't need to be anywhere.

He sat watching the empty park grounds. It was too cold for people to hang out in the park. The leafy trees were mostly bare. The scenery was almost depressing. It was the end of October. Snow had fallen, but melted shortly after. Nature was ready for the long winter sleep. Brooke couldn't stop wondering what was wrong with his friends. How could they suddenly turn on him? Greg had pleaded for him to come back, and now this! He didn't think he treated them badly. As his mind kept questioning his actions, he became fidgety again. He now was annoyed and needed to do something to release the negative energy that invaded his body. He got up, and started running towards the old abandoned warehouse. This retreat was like a second home to him. He slid through the broken window, hidden behind the dumpster, and disappeared inside.

Inside Brooke proceeded to tearing down walls, releasing his anger. He wasn't as careful as he usually tended to be. Everything was coming down so easily. This was exactly what he needed. He punched through the walls with his hammer, and scrapped the crumbling plaster from the lath. Within minutes he was sweating profusely, but he didn't care. Brooke always found relief in hard physical work. His parents always told him he was weak, and would never amount to much. He took pride in contradicting them, but they would never know how limitless Brooke's capabilities were. In his mind, his parents were dead, and he would never see them again. He knew they would never stray from the isolation of their cabin, and he, Brooke, would never go back. The more he thought of his parents, and his friends the more anger he had to release. One day everyone would finally see. He would show them. He would show the world. When and how, he didn't know but he knew it would happen.

Brooke lost track of time when he worked at the warehouse. Hours slipped by. Solitude was a sanctuary for Brooke. His mind would wander. He had big dreams, and he liked to lose himself in those dreams. His daydreams were better than any lullaby.

Once the wall he was working on was completely bare, Brooke started hammering away at the two by fours. Those did not budge easily. They were so old, and had been in place for so long. The nails were square and huge, nothing Brooke had ever seen before. Brooke tried kicking and hammering, but it took a while before it budged only a few millimetres. In his frustration with the lumber, Brooke decided to give a real hard kick. This time the two by four gave so easily that Brooke landed on his back, and the two by four fell right on his face and shoulder. He knew right away that his face would bruise. He could feel his heart beating just below the surface of his skin. The wood had hit hard. He slowly moved his shoulder to see if anything was broken, but luckily he was just sore. He decided that it was time to go home before he hurt himself again, and he needed to get ice on his injuries. Brooke put away his tools, and decided he would clean up the next day. He was too shaken to worry about that right now. Discretely, he left the warehouse, and walked home. After that fall he didn't have the energy to run. He still felt kind of dazed.

As soon as he walked into the house, Brooke headed for the bathroom, and put cold water on his face. His face was throbbing with pain. He took a couple Advils, then hopped in the shower, and went straight to bed with an ice bag on his face. Brooke tossed and turned for half an hour before sleep finally took over. His friends' confrontation still bothered him. What was the big deal if he was late; it wasn't as if they had appointments to keep.

His last thought was; 'The hell with them. Friends were overrated anyway.'

WHAT'S THAT BRUISE DALE?

It was early November now, and a routine had set in. Dale's friendship with Geneva was growing, and he was comfortable with that. They spent a lot of time together, mostly on weekends. She introduced him to the most interesting places in the area. She had a real sense of adventure, and a genuine curiosity about the world. There was an innocence about her that saw the world with a different perspective. She trusted where he didn't. She was courageous in areas where he was frightened. With Geneva Dale discovered many things he never would have discovered on his own. He was too afraid to explore. What struck him most about their friendship was how much they laughed. He had never laughed so much in his entire life. She always did, or said something to make him laugh. Funny enough he was not afraid of being silly around her. Dale had never experienced this kind of ease with anyone before.

Growing up he was mostly a loner. He was rarely around other kids, and when there were other kids around, he was too shy to instigate friendships. Dale believed that he looked too weird for anyone to even want to talk to him. This friendship with Geneva was completely new territory for him, and he was amazed at how easy it was.

That particular morning he had a very embarrassing moment, though. Dale walked out of the house to join Geneva. They walked to campus together every morning. The moment he walked out he saw her face take a weird twist. It seemed to be a mixture of concern and shock. Dale had gotten up late, and had rushed out of the house without looking into the mirror. He felt like a truck had run him over. His muscles were sore, and his face felt swollen.

"What?" he asked as he saw her face take that twist before he had even locked the door.

"What happened to your face?" Her eyes still had that mix of shock and concern, but never turned away from his face.

"What do you mean?" Dale asked completely oblivious.

"You have a black eye, and your cheek is black and blue as well," she didn't stop staring, and her expression didn't lighten either. She was pointing at these areas on his face as she spoke.

"WHAT?" He cried out loud, and ran back into the house to look into the mirror. His face looked like he had been run over by a truck. "Brooke!" He mustered under his breath. He had not noticed, but Geneva had followed him inside the house. She was standing behind him.

"What do you mean?" She asked quietly. She looked scared. "Did he do this to you?" She questioned further as she sat on the bed behind Dale.

"NO! Well, kind of…" He was looking for a way to explain this, but couldn't find the words. Worst of all, he could not tell Geneva the truth. This was his problem, no one else. No one could know. Not ever.

"I can't talk about it Geneva. I'm sorry. Let's go now." Dale walked out of the room, and waited at the door for Geneva to follow. She slowly got up. She looked stunned. He felt so awful seeing her this way. He wanted to tell her the truth, but knew it would be fatal to both Brooke and him. Their secret could never be told. If anyone was ever to find out it would completely destroy them. As much as he trusted Geneva, and he truly believed he could trust her with anything, but this was not something Dale could take a chance with.

Geneva kept glancing at him every few seconds with inquisitive eyes. He could sense anger mixed with concern. Dale knew her well enough now to know the anger was not directed towards him. He was happy that she had never met Brooke, and was likely never to either. Brooke and he stayed away from each others' friends and lives. Everything was black and white with them, no grey areas were allowed.

GENEVA MEETS BROOKE

One Sunday evening, late November, around dinner time, Brooke heard a knock on the front door. Wondering who it might be, he walked over to answer. They never had company so Brooke assumed it was one of these solicitors that go around annoyingly during dinner time to be sure to bug more people. Brooke liked to toy with these people. He usually asked stupid questions, questions a five year old would ask, until they got fed up, and excused themselves. They would suddenly realize they had knocked on the wrong door, and Brooke would close the door behind them laughing his guts out. This time when he opened the door he saw Geneva standing at the door step. He hadn't met her yet.

"Hi! Is Dale here," Geneva inquired with a smile. She was radiant. Her wavy auburn hair fell just below her shoulders. She had beautiful green eyes outlined by heavy black framed glasses. She didn't wear make-up and, with these eyes, really didn't need to.

"No, he isn't. Can I help you?" Brooke replied, curious about how she would react towards him. His mind was racing at a hundred miles an hour, mesmerized by her green eyes.

"Are you Brooke?" she asked.

"Yeah! How d'you know?" Brooke asked somewhat amused. He stood in the doorway posing as if he were on a photo shoot, and smiling back at her.

"I'm a friend of Dale. We go to Lakehead together," she answered still smiling. "We hang out. He told me a little about you."

"Oh! Really? Well, would you like to come in? Dale is out for a while, but we can chill for a bit, if you like," Brooke offered, and moved out of the way to let her in. Now he was curious to see if Geneva could be friends with both, his brother and him. He always envisioned Dale as a mousy, loner type. He never envisioned they could have common friends.

"Sure!" Geneva accepted, and walked in. She had always wondered about Brooke and wasn't about to pass up this opportunity. "I never got to see the place. Dale tells me it's just the two of you." Other than the one time Geneva had followed Dale in to look at his bruised face, she had never been inside. Dale always ran right out, and never even gave her a peek of the place.

"Yeah! We never have anyone over. Kind of a privacy thing, you know."

"I understand. If I had a roommate I wouldn't want all kinds of people coming over either." Geneva was all smiles. She felt some excitement to finally meet Dale's twin brother. He was nothing like she had imagined, neither was their home. Brooke was much friendlier than Geneva had expected, and their home was a lot neater. Brooke dressed trendier than Dale. He wore stylish bold colours. Geneva liked how he spiked his hair. Brooke transpired such self confidence that Geneva could not help but admire him. All these aspects were completely opposite to his brother. With the exception of his friendliness and good manners, which were very much like Dale. His voice, facial and verbal expressions were identical to Dale's. It was almost creepy how identical their physical traits were. Geneva almost had the impression that this was Dale simply clad differently.

Brooke and Geneva sat chatting for a while. Then Brooke suggested they go for a walk. Geneva being so curious, and enjoying Brooke's company graciously accepted.

"So, Geneva, how long have you been in Thunder Bay?" Brooke inquired. He had a real knack for conversation contrarily to his brother.

"Only since June," she replied.

"A newbie, just like us," this piqued Brooke's curiosity. "Where from?" He wanted to know more.

"Deep in the woods," Geneva was very vague. She didn't know Brooke well enough to let out her secrets. She hadn't even shared them with Dale.

"What do your parents think about you being here?" Brooke inquired further. He was now completely intrigued by Geneva's vagueness. He instinctively knew she was hiding something.

"They don't know where I am and I'd like to keep it that way." Geneva looked at the ground as she spoke. "I ran away."

"Really?" Brooke was completely shocked. Geneva didn't look like the type that would run away. She had this goody-two-shoe look about her.

"What happened?" He tried to press further.

"I really don't want to talk about it." Geneva got fidgety.

"Hey! I want to show you something, but you can't tell anyone," Brooke quickly changed the subject. He really liked Geneva, and wanted to share his secret hiding place with her. She had just shared a secret with him so it was only fair that he should share one with her. He knew there was more to her story, but would pry further another day, when Geneva fully trusted him. First, he had to gain that trust. Somehow he felt a strong connection with Geneva. He felt as if he had always known her.

"What is it?" Geneva sounded a little eerie. She didn't know Brooke very well, and from what Dale had told her, he seemed a little wild.

"Don't worry, I'm not going to try anything funny on you," Brooke tried to reassure her. "I found this abandoned warehouse I use as my secret hideaway. It's in an area I like to call 'The Closet of the Forgotten'. Would you like to see it?"

"Sure!" Geneva lightened up. She loved old buildings and secret hideaways.

"But you can't tell Dale about it," Brooke stressed out this last part.

Within half an hour they were crawling through the opening behind the garbage bin.

"It takes a moment for your eyes to adjust," Brooke said casually. "Follow me. I'll show you around." Brooke led Geneva up the stairs, and spent the next fifteen minutes showing Geneva the premises. He showed her where each office had been before he had torn down most of the walls, keeping his favourite for last. Geneva was fascinated. Brooke had done a pretty good job of cleaning the place up. He described the place when he first came, and then explained the improvements he had made. The big office was now as clean as a home. He had fixed and installed the ladder to the bookcase. It still only contained the handful of books he originally found there. Brooke had added a battery operated lamp on a shelf. The desk and chair were nicely polished, and the floor looked brand new. The only improvement Brooke was unable to accomplish was the plastering and painting of the walls. He would have needed supplies. He did not consider it wise to spend money on this place. He knew he could lose his hideaway at any time. A little household cleaning was one thing, but major renovations involving new building materials were too big an investment. The following hour he spent explaining his dreams of one day transforming a place like this into his personal loft. All the while, he couldn't help wonder how Dale and Geneva became friends. Geneva was way too interesting to be a friend of Dales'. So Brooke decided to poke around the subject a little.

"Geneva, could I ask you a personal question?" He slowly attempted.

"Sure! Ask away," Geneva responded with a smile.

"What do you see in Dale? How did you two become friends?" Brooke asked looking genuinely puzzled by the fact.

Geneva's initial response was outright laughter. "Are you serious?" She asked Brooke. "Dale is amazing. He's smart, not pretentious. I'll admit that he is way too shy, but we got past that. Actually, I really enjoy spending time with Dale. He treats me like a human being, and he makes me laugh a lot. Maybe if you spent time with him once in a while you would know that." She was still laughing as she said this. "Now, can I ask you a personal question?" She in turn attempted.

"I guess I do owe you one…" he smirked as he said it.

"Why don't you and Dale ever spend time together?" She didn't know what kind of reaction to expect from that question but she had to ask. Dale had told her about their differences, but after spending time with Brooke, she thought they weren't so different. In fact, she found them to complement each other very well. Instinct told her there was a much deeper reason.

"You're kidding right?" Brooke burst out loud. Geneva simply shook her head indicating that she was dead serious, and the grin on her face indicated she was expecting an answer. Brooke tried the same old tired excuse Dale had given her. They debated the issue for a while then Geneva gave up, promising that she eventually would get to the bottom of this. That comment made Brooke a little uncomfortable. Geneva saw a dark cloud cross over his face, but didn't think much of it.

Shortly after their debate, Brooke walked Geneva home. He invited her out later that week, an invitation that she accepted without hesitation, and they parted with a smile. As Brooke walked into the house, he couldn't help thinking about Geneva, and was bothered by her relationship with his brother. He couldn't say anything to Geneva about it. They knew each other first, and it wouldn't be fair for him to ask Geneva to choose between them. Besides they were only friends.

One Monday morning as Dale walked with Geneva to campus, as their usual routine went. She asked him the following question;

"I went to your house yesterday, but you weren't there. Where did you go?" Her eyes reflected a weird suspicion.

Dale wondered what had brought that on until she added;

"I met your brother," before he could even answer her question. He felt panic overwhelm him as her last words registered into my brain. Did Brooke say anything to tip her off? Did she think he was nice enough to her? Did they talk too much? A million questions and worries were flying at a thousand miles an hour in his head.

"I don't get why you guys don't get along. You are way more alike than either of you care to admit," Geneva continued.

"You talked to my brother?" was all he could say. He felt the blood drain from his head, and could tell he probably looked white as a ghost. Nervously, Dale started flattening his already flat hair with his free hand as he usually did when he got nervous.

"What's wrong with that? Brooke is a pretty cool guy," Dale could tell by Geneva's tone that she was getting defensive. He was convinced that she wondered why he was getting nervous. If she only new the truth, which he could never tell her of course, he knew she would understand his reaction, but he would also probably loose the only friend he ever had.

"Dale, why do you look so nervous?" Geneva looked worried as she spoke. "I actually had a great time with your brother. We're getting together again this week."

"Really? Why?" Dale was really uncomfortable with this new chain of events. He didn't know what kind of repercussions this would have in the future, but it didn't smell right to him. If she got to know both of them too well she would definitely find out the truth. She was too smart not to see it.

They went on with their day as normal, but Dale couldn't help worrying. On the way home he decided to pick Geneva's brain. He wanted to know if she had noticed anything unusual while with Brooke. Had his words or actions compromised their secret in any way?

"So, what kind of stuff did you and Brooke talk about?" He tried to sound cool about it, but he didn't think Geneva was fooled.

"Why are you so bothered about this?" Geneva looked at him with a piercing glare.

"I'm not bothered, just curious," he lied, but again Dale was sure he was busted.

"Yes, you are. I can see right through you, Dale. Your brother is a lot nicer than you make him out to be, you know." She almost looked angry as she said this. Dale almost felt ashamed, but he was also relieved that Geneva had no idea who Brooke really was. Their secret was not compromised, at least not yet.

BROOKE AND GENEVA GET TOGETHER AGAIN

A few days after meeting Brooke, Geneva met up with him after dinner, and they walked together to the secret hideaway. Geneva had put on some old clothes as they had made plans to do some work together in the old warehouse. Geneva was pretty excited, this was the kind of stuff she liked to do, and she had fallen in love with 'The Closet of the Forgotten'. Brooke had shared his theories and views on politics. She agreed with a lot of his perceptions. They made a lot of sense. As they walked they discussed the project for that night. Geneva had agreed to help Brooke tear down the last of the office walls in the warehouse. They wanted to create one large room from the remains of two offices that were set side to side. They weren't sure what they would do with it after, but this was a start. As soon as they got to the warehouse they got to work. Brooke taught Geneva how to crush the plaster with the hammer and scrape it off the lath. They wore scarves over their mouths because this caused a lot of dust, and the smell of the old structure was overwhelming. Once the lath was uncovered they started pulling it out, exposing the old two by four wall structure which they in turn tore down. Together they progressed rapidly. They worked so well together, they barely had to speak. It was as if they could foresee one another's actions, but they did talk; in fact they talked all night long. They talked about everything and nothing discovering many common interests, the night flew by. They both liked individual sports, and had little interest in group activities. They liked to be mentally challenged, and loved to learn new stuff. They were curious about the world. They also needed physical relief, such as running or cycling, and loved to push their bodies to the next level. They felt like two friends that had known each other since kindergarten.

"With so much hunger for knowledge, how come you're not attending University?" Geneva was really intrigued.

"I think its best that Dale gets the education while I work and support us. We could not afford both of us in school at the same time. Besides, I like being self taught. This way I learn what I have interest in, and don't have to study things I really don't give a damn about." Geneva could tell that Brooke was only being half honest. Deep down she was convinced he would have loved to continue his studies further, but was sacrificing for his brother. Geneva admired him for it.

"How do you manage to support the two of you," she asked.

"Don't you know? Hasn't Dale told you?"

"No. Dale never talks about you."

"I'm a bartender at the Voo-Doo Lounge. Money's really good." Brooke went on to telling Geneva stories about his work as they continued the destruction. They pushed all the rubble down the stairs, and into a corner of the main floor. The hours flew by without their knowledge.

Geneva caught the first rays of the rising sun through a window. Distracted by the sight, she did not see the two by four falling towards her. The lumber hit her head, and bounced to the floor. Geneva caught her head in her hands in reaction to the sudden pain. Brooke rushed towards her.

"Sorry! What happened? I didn't realize you weren't ready?" Brooke was trying to apologize. Something that was very difficult for him to do. The panic showed in his eyes as he saw the blood seeping through her fingers and dripping on the floor. "Holy Jumping Jesus! You're bleeding!" Geneva instantly burst out laughing. Brooke looked at her perplexed.

"What are you laughing about," he asked.

Still laughing she managed to say;

"I was picturing Jesus jumping around, and his halo bouncing above his head."

They both burst into laughter. They laughed so much tears rolled down their cheeks. Then Brooke tried to compose himself, remembering that Geneva was hurt. He looked around the room trying to find something to wipe and bandage Geneva's head. He located a roll of paper towels and a bottle of water he had brought. He wet a towel, and proceeded to cleaning Geneva's wound. Luckily it looked worst than it really was. Brooked cleaned the wound as best as he could, which turned out to be only a small cut on the side of her head. Her hair hid it well, but you could tell a bruise was forming under the skin.

"I really should be running home," Geneva finally broke the silence. "I have to get ready for class."

It suddenly hit Brooke as well.

"Holy! Is it morning already?" He looked even more surprised than Geneva had been.

They both hurried out, and ran home. An hour later Geneva was walking to campus with Dale. Dale noticed Geneva kept bringing her hand to her head, and wincing like she had a really bad head ache.

"What's the matter Geneva," he asked.

"Just a headache," she answered. "It'll pass."

"You look pretty pale, you sure you're okay?"

"Yeah! I was up late. That's all." Geneva was quiet. Dale could sense she wasn't telling him everything, but knew not to push her further. Eventually, she would open up. He knew she had seen Brooke again, but felt uncomfortable talking about it. Geneva sensed Dale did not approve of her friendship with Brooke. Honestly, Dale preferred not to hear about it. He had a bad feeling about it. It did make him wonder about her personality. How could she develop a friendship with two people that were so completely different? To him, it didn't make much sense. He decided to bite his tongue about it. This situation would also give him insight into Geneva's true personality.

JUST ONE KISS

A week before Christmas, Brooke and Geneva were sitting together on a park bench. The park was deserted, as it usually happened to be since the cold weather had started. It was also late in the evening, and darkness had taken over. Brooke and Geneva had spent a little time at the warehouse, as they had been every week since they had met almost a month earlier. They had decided to stop in the park on their way home. They were having friendly conversation when suddenly Geneva leaned into Brooke, and stole a kiss from his lips. The move was quick and awkward.

"What the hell?" Brooke yelled as he shot up, and started jumping around. "Why'd you do that?"

Geneva was red as a tomato, "I thought you liked me. And, well, I like you." She answered shyly, blushing profusely.

"Are you crazy?" Brooke couldn't settle down. Of course he liked Geneva, but not in that way. He never thought she would ever try to change the nature of their relationship. What would happen now? "Of course I like you. Actually, I like you so much that I don't want to ruin our friendship with any of that mushy stuff. Did you ever notice what happens to people that bring their friendship to the lovers' level?" Brooke was pacing in front of the bench, flattening his hair with his hands. Geneva was too stunned to notice. "It ends! That's what happens! Do you want our friendship to end?"

"No," her voice was small and hesitant. She was still trying to figure out what was going on. Geneva didn't understand why Brooke was so mad. She never thought that a little kiss could get someone so angry.

"I'm going home." Brooke took off before Geneva could say another word. She sat on the bench for a while longer. She was totally confused. She had really enjoyed Brooke's company and thought he felt the same way about her. She had never kissed a boy before, but she never imagined such a reaction even if her kiss was bad.

Geneva walked home alone. She felt numb. She still could not understand Brooke's reaction, or should she say over reaction. He could have been friendlier about it, and not leave her alone in the dark park, confused and hurt. She started to wonder. Was she not pretty enough for him? She questioned her dressing style, her eyeglasses, everything. Was she too boyish? Did he already have a girlfriend, but had never told her? A million thoughts were racing through her mind. She felt like she'd been led on. They had had a few moments, which she thought meant more than just friendship. Had she misread his intentions? The more she thought about it the more confused she became.

That night Geneva barely slept. She felt a big hole in her chest. Her heart was broken. Every time she started to slip into sleep the events of the night played themselves all over again in her mind like a recurring nightmare. She felt ashamed and stupid. She wished she could turn back the time, and erase that moment forever.

Morning didn't come soon enough, and she felt like a wreck. She considered skipping classes that day, but then figured it would be best to keep her mind busy. She hoped Brooke wouldn't mention anything to Dale. She definitely had no intention of doing so. Besides, she didn't want to hear Dale's thoughts on the subject. She knew Dale would be upset if he found out.

SEASON GREETINGS

"So, what are your plans for Christmas? Geneva just had to ask the question that was on everybody's mind this time of year. Dale never liked these holidays. His parents had never put up a Christmas tree. They thought decorating was a waste of time and money. That was a joke because time was all they had. They never did anything other than drink themselves to oblivion, and money, well they always wasted it on booze anyway. Dale's main pet peeve with Christmas was the commercialization of it. It was insane how it became about buying the love of the people around you. The commercials were insanely annoying and ridiculous. He sometimes wondered how many people were actually gullible enough to fall for most of the commercials. It was everywhere; billboards, television, radio, stores, you name it, and it was there. Being poor made it really depressing. Somehow all the hype around the holiday could make you feel ashamed of being poor, whether you had control over it or not.

If you read the newspapers around this time of year, there were many suicide or murder suicide stories. Christmas had become a very bad time of the year for some people. A lot of depression surrounded these holidays, and there was a reason for that. The true meaning of Christmas had been lost, or never found in the first place, for many.

"I don't know. I haven't given it much thought," Dale answered nonchalantly. He didn't really want to share his dislike of the holidays with Miss Perky, here. "What about you?"

"No plans yet, but I was hoping we could probably do something together. You know, since neither one of us has any family around." Geneva was always so positive about everything. She always had good intentions. Dale had never celebrated Christmas. This would be a first for him. Having been an outcast all his life, he never understood the whole celebration thing.

"What did you have in mind?" He figured it wouldn't hurt to give it a try. Dale knew by the way Geneva asked that it meant a lot to her.

"I was thinking that we could do Christmas dinner at your place. I don't think my landlady would like me entertaining in her kitchen, especially on Christmas day. I'll cook, and we could decorate together. The Dollar Store has a lot of nice Christmas decorations. It wouldn't cost too much money. And we could probably rent a few movies to watch after dinner. What do you say?" As usual, she was all smiles, and her energy was contagious.

"Sure. Why not?" Dale smiled back. "I guess we better start shopping, how about Saturday?"

"Great! I'll start making a list of everything we need, and I'll look up some recipes."

Dale knew right then and there he had made Geneva's day. Her eyes were bright with happiness, and she wore a permanent smile the rest of the day.

The following Saturday, Geneva and Dale had breakfast at his place. They discussed the Christmas meal, selected recipes, and completed the shopping list. They started their day at the Dollar Store, keeping the grocery store for last, and bought four bags full of decorations. Dale had never imagined it would be this much fun. He felt like a kid in a toy store. There was so much choice that he didn't know where to start, where to keep his focus. Thank God Geneva was there, and stopped him from buying too much. He would have easily bought twice as much, but Geneva assured him that they had more than enough. Dale had never been in a Dollar Store before, and was quite surprised at all the things they could get so cheap.

The grocery store was the most expensive. They bought chicken instead of turkey. Dale couldn't believe how huge and expensive turkey was. Geneva was the one to suggest the chicken, assuring him that a turkey would be way too much food for the three of them.

"Three of us?" He turned around, and looked at Geneva, "Are you inviting someone else?"

"No, but isn't Brooke going to be there?" Dale had forgotten that Geneva had met Brooke.

"Oh! Well, no. He has to work that night. It's a really busy night at the Lounge, believe it or not." Dale had to think quickly.

"Ah!" Geneva was obviously disappointed. "Well, I guess it's just the two of us. We'll make sure to make him a plate for when he gets home. Do you know what he's been up to lately? I haven't seen him in a while."

"I really don't know. He pretty much keeps to himself."

Her disappointment was so obvious that Dale found himself trying to justify Brooke's absence further. "Like I said before; we are never in the same room together!" but the more he tried to justify the angrier he got. Dale did not like that Geneva couldn't just respect that Brooke would not be there. Then he realized that his anger was more due to the fear of Geneva discovering the truth than anything else.

"Couldn't you two put your differences aside for one day? You know, that's what Christmas is really about." She was persistent, but had no clue about the truth, and Dale certainly wasn't about to tell her.

"Drop it!" He said with a firm voice. They were silent for a short while, but thankfully Geneva never stayed angry very long, and always knew how to put Dale in a better mood.

For once he was glad that his fridge was almost empty. They were able to freeze the chicken and other meats. He couldn't believe how much food Geneva intended to make. Christmas was the following week, so all the other perishables would keep until Christmas. Geneva intended to start some of the baking the next day.

It was still early so Geneva and Dale got busy with the decorations. Geneva had chosen to put the focus on the red and silver decorations. She said it would go better with all the old fashion furniture that dressed the place. It's true that there were a lot of chrome accents in the furniture, and gold would have looked odd, and red seemed like the more festive choice as their primary colour.

Geneva created a tree with some garlands that she hung together from the ceiling, and then taped each garland to the floor forming a circle. She positioned it in a corner of the living room. There was so little furniture that it wasn't too hard to make space. It was a beautiful illusion, and she even managed to decorate the garlands. Her creativity amazed Dale. She had also brought a bunch of empty boxes that they wrapped with Christmas paper, and placed around their fake tree. It looked beautiful. Dale had to push away the tears. He didn't want Geneva to see his emotional side, too embarrassing.

"Well, the only thing missing is the smell of a natural tree." Geneva stood back admiring her craft.

"Please! I lived with that smell all my life. Quite honestly I don't miss it. I think it's perfect just like that." Dale reassured her.

"Good! I'm glad you like it. I think this will be the best Christmas ever."

"I couldn't agree more."

They hung garlands above the windows and all the doors inside the house, and they even accented the interior windowsills with Christmas lights, which could also be seen from outside.

By mid afternoon they were done, and made plans to start baking the next day. After Geneva was gone Dale had a nap. It had been a busy day. He felt tired.

The next morning Dale woke to the sound of someone pounding on his door. He threw a robe on, and went to the door.

"Aren't you a little early?" He snapped at Geneva.

"I wanted to get an early start, and besides it's not that early. It's ten o'clock, sleepy head."

"You're kidding me." Dale opened the door wider to let Geneva in the house. He couldn't really send her back now. He held his robe closed tightly hoping she didn't notice anything unusual. "Well, come in. If you don't mind, I'm going to have a quick shower before we start."

"Go ahead. I'll start getting organized, and I'll make you coffee and breakfast." Dale was always amazed by how easily Geneva made herself right at home. It didn't trouble him, but rather impressed him.

When Dale got out of the bathroom the smell of coffee, eggs, and toast overwhelmed his senses. His stomach made a loud gurgling sound. Embarrassed and surprised his eyes opened wide. Geneva looked up at him, also with a surprised look on her face. Instantaneously they burst out laughing.

"I guess that means you're hungry," said Geneva. "That's good because everything is ready."

They sat down, and ate. There was never a dull moment when Dale was with Geneva. They talked, and laughed, and talked, and laughed some more. That day they baked some sugar cookies, and tried to make some shortbread cookies. The shortbread cookies didn't quite come out right; they were hard as a rock. Those ended up in the garbage. They also made meat stew, and roasted the ham and pork. The house felt homier with the scent of all the baked food. Dale had never experienced this kind of comfort before.

Geneva and Dale reviewed the recipes for the courses that they would be cooking the following Friday. Geneva wanted to be sure they weren't missing anything, and if they were that they could get it before then. She gave Dale instructions to thaw the meats the day before, along with a few other preparations that would alleviate their schedule on the Friday. Geneva had exams on the Thursday while Dale was off, and free to do some of this stuff.

Christmas day came quickly. Before Dale knew it, Geneva and he were sitting in the living room, their bellies full. Dale felt like a fat cat who had just feasted on a family of mice.

They were sitting in the living room about to exchange gifts. They had not planned it, but both had gotten each other a gift.

Dale waited while Geneva opened hers. He could see from her expression that she had not expected to receive a gift, and was very pleased. She removed the silk bow from around the box then slowly removed the paper, ever so careful not the rip it. She was so cautious that it was torture waiting to see her reaction. She finally opened the box. Her eyes were looking inside as her hand completely removed the lid. Then to Dale's surprise tears come rolling down her cheeks. This was one reaction he had not anticipated.

Embarrassed, he asked; "Is it that bad?"

"No!" She said tears rolling down her cheek. "It's that good. I love it!"

"Then why are you crying?"

"Because I'm so happy, and this is the most thoughtful gift I ever received." As Geneva said this, she removed the picture frame from the box. Inside the frame was a picture of the two of them at the Fort William Historical Park.

Geneva gave Dale a scarf she had knitted herself. He was amazed by her talent, and by how personal it made the gift. That moment they shared made him realize how strong their friendship truly was. For the first time in his life he felt the true meaning of Christmas. At that moment he saw Geneva as an angel who had come to teach him some of the most important lessons in life. The most important was 'How to live', truly live, and cherish the moments that were important such as this one.

A BODY IS FOUND

It was a cold January day. Snow covered every non-traffic surface. The roads were slushy, and you could hear the swooshing of the motor vehicles traveling nearby. Brooke was heading to his usual hideaway when he spotted trouble ahead.

The normally quiet 'Closet of the Forgotten' was peppered with flashing emergency lights. Blocks from Brooke's hideaway, all the roads were closed. Yellow tape was blocking access behind the police cars. A Forensics Police Investigation truck was parked in front of the abandoned warehouse, where Brooke liked to go collect his thoughts.

Brooke wondered what could possibly have happened. He had been there the night before, and had not noticed anything unusual. The regular bums hung around the trash bins, hovering over some shopping carts, or balled up in cardboard boxes.

He couldn't believe his eyes when he saw a body bag dragged out of the warehouse. He was observing the scene from a distance; he had climbed up the fire escape ladder of a nearby building. 'Now what?' he thought to himself.

After a while, Brooke decided to go back home, hoping to find out more on the news. He turned on the black and white television to a local station the instant he walked into the house. As he took off his coat, eyes glued on the tube, the anchor started talking about a dreadful discovery in an abandoned warehouse located in a closed industrial park.

"This Industrial Park has been closed for almost thirty years, and is now a hideout for local homeless people," the anchor continued to say.

A local bum alerted the police, and guided them to the warehouse where the inert body was found. The deceased, a white female in her late teens or early twenties, they believed had died from natural causes. Police were still investigating. The identity of the victim was still unknown, and police urged anyone with information to come forward.

Brooke slumped on the couch heavily, discouraged and scared. He wondered if the cops would trace anything back to him. He had spent a lot of time there, his fingerprints were all over the place, and he had left tools and other belongings there. The police were bound to track him down. Then his thoughts hinged on Geneva. He put his coat back on, and ran across the street.

During this time at the station, the man who had found the body was giving his statement. He and the deceased had observed a young man coming in and out of the warehouse over the last six months. They had watched him coming sometimes early in the evening Sunday to Wednesday, and sometimes late at night usually from Thursday to Saturday. They had seen him almost every day. Once they had figured out his schedule, they had started going in themselves for the comfort of the shelter. They, the bum and the deceased, always made sure they left before the unknown man came back. They also made sure not to leave any traces. They didn't want him suspecting their presence during his absence.

"Did you ever notice any one else coming to this warehouse," asked the officer interrogating.

"Yeah! He brought a girl with him a few times," the bum seemed to be digging into his memory. His dirty fingers rubbing his forehead, which was just as soiled. The man obviously had not bathed for several months. His clothes would probably stand on their own if they were removed from his body. The police officer tried hard to ignore the stench coming off the guy.

"What did she look like?" the officer pushed further.

"Kind of the same height as me. Skinny, like a ballerina. White skin." The bum answered in a shaky rough voice, a heavy smoker's voice. He seemed to be having trouble concentrating, and his breath reeked of alcohol.

"How about the colour of her hair and eyes?" said the officer, probing further.

"I don't know," the bum was almost in tears. "We always looked from a distance. Why did my Mia die?" pleaded the bum, suddenly agitated as if momentarily reminded that he had lost his friend.

"That's what we are trying to find out, but it seems her health wasn't very strong. Was your friend sick?" The cop tried to sound sympathetic.

"How could you not be sick on the street in this cold hell?" The bum got agitated and started to cry, resting his head in his hands on the table.

"You must have seen the hair," the officer insisted.

"She always had a baseball cap on," the bum continued to sob.

Sensing he wouldn't get any further while the man was upset. The officer left the room coming back a few minutes later offering a cup of coffee to the bum. The man took it without a word. His eyes transpired gratefulness for the kind action. It was obvious that he wasn't use to kindness. Half an hour later they let the bum go.

During this time, crime scene investigators screened the whole warehouse. They collected fibres, hairs, and anything else they could find. A full autopsy was scheduled. The team had a lot of work on their hands. The old dusty warehouse had collected a lot of DNA samples through the years. They had to eliminate the old ones and the animal or vermin DNA from the human in order to narrow down their evidence, and concentrate on the case at hand.

Over the following forty-eight hours, they analyzed every hair, skin particle, footprint, bloodstain, and fibres collected at the scene. The samples indicated the recent presence of four people. Three were female and one male. They confirmed the male to be the bum who had reported the body, and one of the females was the deceased. This left them with two unidentified females. They ran the DNA samples through the system. A few days later, they identified only one of the two. Christa Makins, this girl was on the missing persons list from the OPP North East Region Department in Sault Ste. Marie. Her parents had died in a house fire in June of the previous year. According to the quantity of samples linked to her DNA she had spent a lot of time in that warehouse. Her presence in that warehouse became an even greater mystery. Many questions ran through the team's minds. How did this girl from Echo Bay end up in an abandoned warehouse in Thunder Bay? Did someone abduct her, and bring her there? Was she still alive? Was the fire really accidental, or had someone caused it to hide an abduction? So many questions arose with the new discovery of Christa Makins' DNA. All resources had to be pooled in order to find the missing girl. Therefore, they contacted the department hoping to get pictures and all available information.

Thunder Bay Police were hoping to get a lead, but no pictures of Christa Makins were available. All they got was a sketch of the girl created from the descriptions acquired from the Sault Ste. Marie Mid-City Motel owner for whom they believed she worked and the Echo Bay grocery store owners. The investigation had revealed very little people knew the Makins family, making it much harder to find the missing girl. Finding Christa Makins was the first key the police needed in order to solve this case. Although it was confirmed that the loafer had died of natural causes the DNA discovery brought a completely different twist to the case. It was no longer about the deceased, but now about finding the missing girl.

Police plastered every post and every wall in Thunder Bay and surrounding towns with the sketch of Christa's face. Every television station broadcasted her story. Still no one around seemed to know her. No one in this part of the country had ever seen or heard of Christa Makins.

As the investigator in charge went through the file, he noticed a discrepancy. He made his way to the lab.

"Charlie, something doesn't jive with the warehouse case," he told the analyst.

"What do you mean?" Charlie's eyes squinted as he turned to face Officer Carnell.

"Your DNA file indicates the presence of three females and only one male in the warehouse, the male being our witness. Who in turn claims having observed another male going into that warehouse regularly."

"I'll check again, but I am pretty sure no mistake was made. I was very careful." Charlie took the file from Carnell, and went back to work.

Carnell tried to piece the puzzle together. Why would DNA only show one male and three females when it should be two and two. There had to be a mistake.

NEW DEVELOPMENTS

The next day, January 16ᵗʰ, 2005, the telephone rang in a high rise, Chicago penthouse.

"Ms. Reese, please," a male voice rang through the phone.

"This is she," Rebecca Reese responded. Every time the phone rang she hoped it was news about her niece. Even though it had been more than six months, she still hoped to find her alive. Rebecca Reese wanted to give Christa a better home and chance in life. She dreamed of giving her niece the best education money could buy, and teach her about the nicer things in life. Teach her that not all was evil in this world. She only knew too well how much Christa suffered growing up with alcoholic parents living deep in the woods remote from civilisation. She feared the emotional scars that might haunt the poor girl. The sooner she could find her, the sooner she could help her heal.

"Ms. Reese, my name is Detective Inspector Chris Carnell from the Criminal Investigation Bureau. Detective Constable James Clarke from OPP North East Region in Sault Ste. Marie provided me with your missing niece's file. May I ask you a few questions?" The Inspector's tone was very formal. Rebecca couldn't read into it. She didn't know whether to expect good or bad news.

"Of course Inspector, have you found her?" Rebecca was hopeful. She could feel excitement building despite herself. She didn't want to get her hopes up too quickly, but couldn't help it.

"Not really, Ms. Reese, but we do know that she has been and might still be in Thunder Bay, which brings me to my first question. Do you have any relatives or acquaintances in this area that Christa might have come to visit?"

"No, not that I know of, my sister and I had not spoken in over sixteen years. I wouldn't know of any acquaintances." Rebecca's heart sank. She wished she could have known these things. "Inspector Carnell, you say she might still be in Thunder Bay, does this mean you have a lead?"

"A small one, but I can not discuss it. It is confidential at the moment. Is there anything you can think of that might have drawn your niece to this city?" insisted the Inspector.

"I wish I did, but unfortunately I really have no idea. I did not know my niece, but I am hoping to change that the moment we find her." Carnell could hear the heavy emotions in Rebecca's voice. He would have much preferred to call her with the news she had been hoping for. "You will keep me posted with any new developments, right?"

"Absolutely! I have no other questions at the moment, but should you think of anything, please call me." Inspector Carnell gave Rebecca his coordinates then hung up the phone. He was no further ahead than before, and was getting tired of all these dead ends.

The moment Rebecca disconnected with Inspector Carnell, she called Higgleton. Higgleton was the private investigator she had hired to find Christa. He had also only found dead ends, but not yet given up. He refused to give up.

"Hi! It's Rebecca Reese calling. The Criminal Investigation Bureau just called me. They think she might be in Thunder Bay," Rebecca told Higgleton. Higgleton asked a few questions. Rebecca answered best she could. The conversation terminated, Rebecca went to the kitchen, and made tea. Her mind was wandering. She didn't know whether to be hopeful or fearful. The Inspector had been so formal she couldn't tell if his lead was positive or negative. Did they know if she was alive or dead? Questions kept taunting her, but no answers were available to soothe her worries.

Meanwhile in Canada, Higgleton was already heading for Thunder Bay. He had packed, and left less than half an hour after hanging up with Ms. Reese. In his line of work one had to always be prepared to leave on a moments notice. As he drove he was mentally planning his investigation in Thunder Bay.

His first visit would be to the Thunder Bay Police Department. Although, it had been the CIB (Criminal Investigation Bureau) that had called Rebecca Reese, Higgleton knew that Thunder Bay Police would still have someone of their own working with the CIB on the case. Because Christa Makins had disappeared from Echo Bay, and then a lead had been found in Thunder Bay, a Detective Inspector from the Criminal Investigation Bureau was assigned to coordinate the investigation between the OPP North East Region and the Thunder Bay Police Department. This was all standard procedure.

Higgleton intended on finding out what information Thunder Bay Police had regarding Christa. He still had a few contacts there from his RCMP days. 'Hopefully this will not be another dead end,' he thought to himself.

Later that evening, Higgleton sat on his hotel bed and read a copy of the file on Christa Makins. He would never have gotten access to this file, but his contact in the Thunder Bay Police Department knew Higgleton well. He knew Higgleton was discrete, and if anything, Higgleton would help crack the case.

As Higgleton read the file, he discovered the only lead Thunder Bay Police had was Christa's DNA found in an abandoned warehouse. This is where he would start the following day. He intended on searching the surrounding area for any clues. He hoped he could find something that local police might have missed. After watching an hour of mindless television, Higgleton turned down for the night. He wanted to get an early start the next day.

The following morning Higgleton was at the warehouse around six o'clock. He wanted to explore. He started by walking around the warehouse, observing everything and everyone around. He noticed all the homeless people sheltered by cardboard boxes in inconspicuous corners, or strolling around with shopping carts full of other peoples' garbage which became their treasures. As he made his way around the warehouse he noted that a broken window behind a garbage bin in the back alley was the only way in. He discretely slid into the warehouse observing possible witnesses. No one seemed to be paying much attention to him, most were asleep, and others simply kept to their own business. Their tired eyes were either closed, or looking in a different direction.

Once inside, he stood still letting his eyes adjust to the dimness of his surroundings. He took in the open space with the staircase in the middle of the place leading to a second floor. He could see the police markings of the deceased and the identification pegs left behind by CSI. He carefully made his way to the staircase. From what he could see of the main level, not much activity, other than the bums hanging around, the scavenging of rats or cats, and the recent police investigation, had occurred in this part of the warehouse for a very long time. His gut told him that he would find better clues upstairs. He slowly made his way up, careful not to disturb anything. He was glad that the cold weather called for gloves. He would not have liked to touch the old grimy hand rail with his bare hands, and didn't want to leave clues of his presence behind either. At the top of the stairs, the sun sneaked through some cracks in the window boards, letting in slightly more light. He stood in place for at least ten minutes just observing every detail visible from that position. Higgleton was startled when a cat ran past him up the stairs, and headed directly through the double doors at the end of the hall, and disappeared into the room.

It was obvious that someone had put a lot of effort in trying to clean up the place, and even attempted renovating. He made a mental note that he should check the ownership of the building. In his search, Higgleton found tools hidden in a corner covered by a tarp. He also noticed the cat lying in a brand new basket with her kittens, and next to it were two bowls for food and water, now empty. Someone was being careful not to be discovered, he assumed from the way the tools were placed and covered. He looked around for a bag of cat food, which he found on a shelf in the built-in bookcase. He filled the cats' bowl, and poured water from his bottle he had in his coat pocket. Something else was nagging at him. Something just wasn't quite right. According to his info, a witness declared seeing a man coming to the warehouse regularly, but things were too neat. Something didn't jive. Also the DNA reports did not indicate the presence of a man other than the witness himself. This, he felt, was a very important piece of the puzzle. The P.I. walked around the second floor at least twenty times, following different directions and patterns. He didn't want to miss anything. He always kept in mind that sometimes the most insignificant looking clue is the key to the whole mystery. He was looking for that key.

Back outside, Higgleton started walking every street around the warehouse. Creating a huge spiral of about two kilometres in diameter, the neighbourhood didn't offer much, it had been abandoned for over thirty years, but he thought that might be another clue.

After his search of the warehouse premises Higgleton headed for city hall. He needed to know who's building that was. The hard part was that he did not have an address. All the street names had been removed in that odd area. None of the buildings bore any signs. No clues were left to what their purpose had once been.

At City Hall in the records department Higgleton searched all the maps, but nothing existed with that area showing as an industrial park. The maps only portrayed government owned vacant land. It was as if someone had wiped out all traces of its existence. He tried to pry information out of some of the older employees, but they simply clammed up. Everyone acted weird, and all insisted they had no idea what he was talking about.

Now, it was time to go back to the police department. He had a few questions he wanted to ask his old friend Jack. Maybe he would know a thing or two about this mysterious area and this warehouse in particular.

THE ARREST

February waltzed right in, and according to the newspapers, police had ruled the death of the woman to be natural. It had already been a month since the gruesome discovery. Brooke had kept a close eye on all the papers and news broadcasts. He was eager to go back to his sanctuary, and was waiting for the coast to be clear. He wondered what the cops might have found or concluded from all the work he had done in the place. From careful observation, he noticed police activity in and around the warehouse had ceased three weeks earlier. Brooke felt pretty confident.

As he walked down the streets Brooke took a few detours to his destination, looking for any clues of police activity. Not that he knew exactly what to look for. Once he was satisfied that no cops were watching, and that everything was back to normal. The bums were back to their usual hiding spots, shivering in the cold of winter. Some dug caves in the snow banks in hope of some warmth. Brooke was always amazed that these people could survive in such a climate. He really felt sorry for them but he didn't want his hideaway to turn into a crack house, or another disgusting, illegal hang out for the junkies of Thunder Bay. He had seen other warehouses taken over that way by society's vampires, and turned into profitable locations for the drug dealers and pimps. No way would he let his secret place be taken away from him. He needed this place to collect his thoughts and keep his sanity, his home away from home.

He slid behind the usual dumpster, which thankfully the police had not removed, and through the broken window into the warehouse. The moment he got inside he felt something was different. He felt a presence. It took a moment for his eyes to adjust to the darkness, but then it was too late.

"Put your hands up!" An authoritative voice yelled out. Four cops surrounded Brooke walking out of the dark corners of the warehouse. Their guns pointed at him. Brooke had no choice but to comply. This wasn't good.

"We knew you'd come back. No one puts this much effort and just leaves it behind," said one of the cops. Brooke only heard half of what the officer said, and didn't know which of the four had spoken. The moment he saw them everything around him became a blur. He stood with his hands up, and let the cops handle him without any resistance. Brooke was overwhelmed with a multitude of feelings, but could not identify a single one. He could not describe this moment even if he tried. Confused, angry, scared were just a few of the things he felt and all these feelings were so tightly wound that the feelings became unrecognizable.

Once at the station, they dragged him to a small room containing only a table and two chairs. He sat alone there for what seemed like hours. He knew he was being watched from the other side of the, supposedly, mirror. He had seen it in movies and on television. How was he going to get himself out of there? He couldn't risk the consequences of jail.

While frisking him, the cops had found the money belt around his waist. Brooke knew they would want an explanation for this. Never, did he think that his precautions would end up putting him into trouble.

Another officer walked in. Brooke had not seen this officer before. He was a tall tough looking cop. The one they send in to rattle your cage, he assumed, also from some movies he had seen.

"What were you doing in that warehouse," was the first question they asked Brooke in the interrogation room. This room was cold and uncomfortable. The intimidating white walls reflecting the fluorescent lights from the ceiling made the steel table and chairs feel even colder.

"Just hanging out," Brooke replied. He hoped the truth would get him out quickly. He really wasn't doing anything illegal.

"Who else hung out with you there?" they followed.

"No one," Brooke didn't want to tell the cops about Geneva. She had confided in him about her runaway status. He understood what could be involved in her being found.

"Where is Christa Makins," the cop asked. This question really took Brooke by surprise.

"Who?" Brooke responded bewildered.

"How do you know Christa Makins?" The cop tried again.

Brooke felt his blood rushing through his whole body. He hoped it wasn't too apparent.

"Come on. We know she has been spending time in that warehouse. I doubt you didn't know that." The cop was very persistent about Brooke knowing this girl.

Brooke couldn't find the words to say next, his face felt hot, and his hands were clammy. He felt that if he didn't get out straightaway, he would be sick or faint. He felt like a wild animal trapped in a cage. He knew this arrest could be the end of Dale and himself.

"One more question, and I want a straight answer on this one." The cop looked at him straight in the eyes, his voice was authoritarian, but not threatening. "What's the story with the money belt?"

"I don't trust banks," Brooke said without flinching, looking the cop defiantly straight in the eyes.

"Ever hear of a safe?" the cop continued, still holding eye contact with Brooke.

"I don't trust people either," Brooke said in an even tone.

"Where did you get the money?"

"I earned it."

"How?"

"Bartending."

"Bartending pays that well, does it? Maybe I should reconsider my career choice." The cop said mockingly.

"That money is what I put aside over a few years," Brooke responded, angry now by the fact the cop had mocked him. He worked hard, and didn't like anyone belittling his efforts. The cop turned around without another word, and left the room.

Brooke spent the next few hours between interrogations, and time alone. He knew that during his time alone cops were watching him from the other side of the mirror, waiting for him to break down. Brooke had to keep control of every fibre of his being not to betray his secret.

Every now and then Brooke would feel his mind slipping. He had to muster every bit of his energy to stop the phenomena. His head was pounding from the stress of being trapped in this box. He felt like the room was closing in on him. Everything started to look unreal to him.

It was as if he was watching a movie. A migraine crept its way into his brain. It was suddenly so powerful he had to hold his head with both hands. He pushed his palms into his eye sockets trying to relieve some of the pressure. His head grew so heavy he couldn't hold it up any longer. Brooke rested his forehead on the table, eyes shut tight, but he could still feel the light piercing into his brain. He felt like he was in a bubble sinking deep under water. The voices sounded muffled; words no longer made sense to him. He tried to speak, but he couldn't even pronounce the simplest words. He slurred rather than spoke. One of the cops looked at him, and noticed how white Brooke's face suddenly looked.

"Okay Guys, let's give him a break before he faints." They walked out of the room leaving Brooke alone. The cop who had suggested the break turned the light off as he walked out of the room. He was a migraine sufferer himself, and had recognized the signs.

Brooke fell asleep almost instantly, but woke only a few minutes later. He opened his eyes, but the room was completely dark, adding to his disorientation. Then he remembered he was still at the police station. This wasn't a dream. The sympathetic cop that had given him the earlier break walked in, turning on only one of the light switches. The light hit Brooke's eyes harshly, but he was thankful that the cop had been considerate in turning on the minimum lighting possible.

"Okay kid you can go for now, but we'll be watching your every step. Don't go thinking about skipping out on us because we'll be right behind you, and then you will have to stay in jail until we sort out this mess." The cop then brushed his hand indicating to Brooke to leave the room.

Detective Inspector Carnell later looked at the report of Brooke's interrogation. He read it twice over to make sure he hadn't missed anything then called on the cops who had done the interrogation into his office.

"Rick, I don't see anything about a DNA sample being taken from the kid," he questioned.

"We didn't think you needed one, sir. Since our unidentified suspects are all female..." Rick looked worried as he replied.

"I still want a DNA sample from this kid. Did you get his name and address at least?"

Detective Inspector Carnell gave the order to get a DNA sample from Brooke as soon as possible. He then went over the whole file of the warehouse case over again. He had read this file at least a hundred times, but he couldn't shake the feeling that he was missing something obvious. As the saying went 'Sometimes you can't see what is right in front of you'. He knew the clue was there, but he just couldn't figure it out.

It was now evening, the time when most kids Brooke's age were out and about. Detective Inspector Carnell decided he would go ask around about Brooke. After hitting a few different cafés and pubs, he finally hit the 'jack pot'. He found some guys who knew Brooke and proceeded to questioning them.

"We all knew he needed his head checked but to kill someone… no! He could never do that!" Josh was telling the police. Josh didn't always get along with Brooke, but deep down he didn't think Brooke capable of murder. "I thought the paper said that the girl had died from natural causes. What does Brooke have to do with anything?" Detective Inspector Carnell ignored Josh's question, and continued his interrogation.

"How about Christa Makins, do you know her," the officer proceeded to ask Josh.

"Who? No, I never heard that name before. Who is she," Josh asked in return. Confusion showed in his face at the mention of that name. It was quite obvious that this name meant nothing to him. "Wait! Isn't that the girl from the posters and on the news?"

"Yes, she's a missing girl from Echo Bay. She is about the same age as you guys. You sure you never met her?" Carnell explained and inquired again.

Carnell asked Peter and Greg all the same questions. After about an hour Detective Inspector Carnell left. He was no further ahead than before he spoke to those kids. Something was really amiss. Even his own friends didn't seem to know him well. "What are you hiding Brooke?" Carnell asked himself out loud. He heard footsteps behind him and turned to see Greg running after him.

"Officer! Can we have a word privately," Greg asked, slightly out of breath. "I really don't know if this will help but I feel like I should tell you."

Greg proceeded to telling the officer about the time he saw Brooke talking to himself.

"I only heard Brooke's voice and saw no one else standing there." Gregory was telling the officers, "It was as though he was having a conversation with himself".

"Are you sure that no one was standing in the shadows or anywhere hidden," the officer inquired.

"I'm positive," Gregory sounded slightly desperate, "he was standing in the middle of the park with no trees or anything close enough to conceal anyone. Officer I truly believe Brooke needs help. He is no criminal, but he gets weird sometimes."

"What do you mean by weird?"

"He gets really paranoid sometimes, as if he thinks everyone is watching him, or conjuring some type of scheme against him. I really don't know how to explain it." Greg was hoping he was doing the right thing by telling the cop this.

"Do you know where he is now?"

"No, he stopped hanging out with us a few months ago. I go see him at work every now and then, but he has been keeping to himself lately." Gregory was worried about Brooke as he told Detective Inspector Carnell about the change in attitude.

"Thanks, kid. Here's my card. If you think of anything else, please call." Carnell left, and Greg went back into Starbucks. As he reached his friends he saw the interrogative eyes upon him.

"Hey! Greg. What do you make out of this Makins girl? Where does she fit into this picture?" Josh asked his friend. They were trying to figure out who this Makins character could be.

"I have no idea, never heard the name before. You?" Greg asked both Josh and Peter.

"Me neither" responded Peter. He looked just as flabbergasted as his peers. All three sat in silence for a while. Even a stranger could tell that they were truly concerned and perplexed. They didn't like the fact that their friend was in trouble. Although, Brooke was somewhat difficult at times, they still cared for him.

"I think I should pay him a visit at work tomorrow," Greg said to his friends. They all nodded in agreement.

A RESEMBLANCE

Following the information gathered from the Thunder Bay Police, Higgleton had spent a few days watching Dale and Brooke's house. This was the only lead he had at the moment. The police had found out about the twins while interrogating Brooke's friends. Higgleton had a feeling these boys held the key to finding Christa. He couldn't exactly explain it yet, but his gut told him there was more here than what was seen from the outside world.

From the description he had of Brooke, he noted no action from this party. Instead, he had observed a geeky guy walking with a young girl, of whom he noted the resemblance with Christa Makins, and thought, 'this is it, this girl walking with the geeky guy to Lakehead University every day has to be Christa'.

Her hair was a different colour, but she easily could have coloured it. She had a slim boyish body, as described by the few people who might have known Christa. They both had fair skin, and the eyewear; he suspected might be a decoy. There were just too many resemblances, which he could not ignore. Without an actual picture it was hard to be sure. He truly believed in the possibility that this girl could be Christa incognito. He had to find an opportunity to investigate these suspicions further. He had to talk to her. He was waiting for an opportunity to ask her a few questions that might confirm his suspicions.

Finally, one evening in early March, Geneva walked out of the house, and started to walk east on Andrew Street. Higgleton drove to the next block. He got out of his car, then walked towards her, and introduced himself. He explained that he was investigating the disappearance of Christa Makins. He carefully watched Geneva's reaction to the name of Christa Makins. She didn't show any sign of disturbance at the name. Higgleton concluded she either, was a really good actress, and had been expecting this question, or had absolutely no clue as to who Christa was. He showed Geneva a sketch of Christa, and asked if she had ever seen the girl. Geneva's initial reaction was a sudden gasp. Higgleton was satisfied with this break in her reaction and immediately thought his first conclusion was the correct one. Geneva recomposed herself, and with calmness in her voice answered;

"No, but does she have any relatives? Brothers, cousins, anything?" Geneva asked. She frowned as she stared at the sketch.

"Not that we know of, why do you ask?" Higgleton was rather surprised by the question.

"Well, she kind of looks like Dale and Brooke," she said still staring at the sketch, turning the sheet around in every angle. She blocked the long hair with her free hand trying to get a better perspective.

"This is so weird. They must be related," Geneva added. The detective thought that she was probably trying to turn the focus off her, and on to the boys. Higgleton studied Geneva's expression as she stared at the picture. He tried to read her eyes. He had been trained to notice every little detail of a person's demeanour.

He couldn't let her know that he knew who the boys were so he asked the question. Geneva then went on to explaining how she had met Dale at Lakehead, and then Brooke while Dale had been out one day.

"How well do you know them?" Higgleton asked. He needed to get as much information without causing suspicion, or scaring her away.

"Well, Dale and I are best friends. We hang out a lot. We walk to campus together everyday. As for Brooke, we spent a little bit of time together up until a week or so before Christmas." Geneva's expression changed as she said the last sentence, sadness could be read in her eyes.

"We had a disagreement. Then I never saw or heard from him again. Dale refuses to talk about him."

"Did you spend time with him in an old warehouse?" Higgleton hoped her answer would confirm his suspicions about her identity.

"Yes, I went there with him a few times but please don't tell the police about me." Higgleton noticed fear in Geneva's eyes. 'This has to be her,' he thought to himself.

"Are you in trouble? Does it have anything to do with the body that was found?" He attempted. Hoping this would get her to elaborate.

Geneva stood there shifting her weight from foot to foot. Her eyes were looking around wildly. She looked very uncomfortable. Finally she looked Higgleton straight in the eyes.

"I'm a runaway," she said in a matter of fact manner, "but my parents are horrible. I can't go back. As for the warehouse, I hadn't been there in over a month when that body was found. You don't think Brooke had anything to do with it, do you?" Her eyes were tearing up. Higgleton immediately noticed the fear.

"Don't worry I won't say anything about your status, and no, Brooke had nothing to do with that girls' death. This stays between us, but I will need your cooperation with something though," Higgleton reassured her, and went on to explaining what he needed from her. Still not wanting to arouse her suspicion, and not to let on that he thought *she* was Christa Makins, Higgleton decided to act as if he was simply following the police's trail.

"Do you know where Brooke is?"

"No, and Dale won't tell me either. You see, the guys don't get along. They actually never spend anytime together. Dale is the day person while Brooke is the night guy. You never see them together. It's really weird," Geneva shrugged as if a breeze had blown up her spine.

"Can we walk as we talk? I have some errands to run and I don't want to miss store hours." Geneva started walking even before Higgleton could answer. Since he still wanted to chat with her, he simply fell into step.

"I'm sorry. Sure. I could always use a good walk," he answered in the same action. "Could you tell me more about them?"

Geneva told Higgleton everything she knew about the twins, their differences, their similarities, their opinions of each other. The more he heard, the stranger the story became. Something wasn't right, but he couldn't put his finger on it. They continued to talk as they walked to the store, and back to his car. Geneva continued the short distance from Higgleton's car to her home, alone. This interview with Geneva had Higgleton somewhat reassured he was on the right track. Yet, he couldn't shake the feeling that he was still missing something. He brushed that last feeling thinking it was time to retire, which he intended to do after this case was solved. Part of him was convinced that Geneva was Christa in hiding, but a little nagging voice inside contradicted him. One way or another, he would find out the next day when DNA results came from the lab. No sense in driving himself crazy until then.

IS IT A MATCH?

Higgleton had made arrangements with Geneva to get her DNA sample, promising to keep her identity anonymous. He used the excuse of wanting to clear her from the scene. In order to gain her trust, he had also promised that her whereabouts would remain unknown to the police, and that the most her family would get is a note stating her well-being, telling them to stop searching for her. Besides, she was of age to lawfully refuse to live with her parents. Higgleton knew the system would support her decision once they heard about the abuse. From what he gathered from Rebecca Reese, the parents were real losers and boozers. Higgleton was convinced that Geneva William was Christa Makins in hiding. He was now just waiting for the DNA results to confirm it.

At the Thunder Bay Police Station, Higgleton walked directly to Jack McKellar's desk.

"Hey Jack! I got something for you to check." Higgleton tossed a container to his Thunder Bay police acquaintance.

"What is this," Jack asked.

"Just check it against the warehouse samples, and then call me with the results."

Higgleton walked out. Jack knew him well enough not to ask any questions, at least not yet. Jack McKellar and Higgleton had worked together on a murder case some twenty years ago. At the time, McKellar had witnessed a strong instinct within Higgleton. Higgleton had almost single-handedly led the team straight to the killer. From then on, whenever McKellar dealt with Higgleton, he just followed his lead, and asked questions later. They had cooperated on several cases since, McKellar had never seen Higgleton make a mistake. Higgleton always made sure he had all the facts before pronouncing himself.

A few hours later, Jack got a call from the CSI team regarding the sample Higgleton had brought in. His discussion was brief, but the results were startling. Larry had to call Higgleton quick. Now he had questions to which he needed answers. Jack called Higgleton, and made a lunch appointment with him. This conversation had to take place outside the department, or he knew he wouldn't get any answers from Higgleton. He also couldn't let it be known that he was cooperating with Higgleton. McKellar was breaking protocol, but he knew that Higgleton could help with this case. They had no clue where to look. That Reese kid had disappeared before they could get his DNA sample. Higgleton was a loyal friend, and great law enforcement officer. Even after leaving the RCMP Higgleton had always been on the right side of the law, he sometimes broke protocol when it got in the way, but the end result was always worth it.

As Jack McKellar walked into the diner, Higgleton spotted him, and waved him over.

"You haven't changed Jack," Higgleton said as the man sat in front of him. "I must have uncovered important information for you to call a meeting outside the station." Higgleton immediately inquired about the case. "So? Are you going to tell me we have a match?" Higgleton stared at Jack, a sly smile on his face.

"Yes, but…" Jack left the information in suspension for a few minutes. Higgleton could tell that Jack was uncomfortable with what he had to tell him. "First, I have to ask you a few questions about how you got that sample."

"I promised her she would remain anonymous," he immediately informed him. "Anything you want to know has to go through me."

Jack pressed his lips together. He looked down at his hands resting on the diner table. He looked up at Higgleton. McKellar's eyes were tired, and full of sadness. He had been on the force for a long time, and seen too much shit. He knew what people were capable of, and knew that if Higgleton was protecting this girl it was with good reason.

"I will agree to that for now, but you know I'm putting my ass on the line by sitting here with you. I gave you privileged information, and I am currently withholding information from the investigative team. If the department finds out, I'm history."

"Don't worry. I have it almost solved. The information you give them will make you a hero. Now can we get back to the reason we're here?" Jack gave Higgleton a nod. "Did the DNA match any from the warehouse?" Higgleton was eager to know. If this was the match he expected then he could start his retirement the following week after reuniting Rebecca Reese with her niece.

"Yes, but I'm not sure it's the match you're hoping for," McKellar said. "The DNA matches the unidentified female, not Christa Makins'."

"Come again," Higgleton couldn't believe his ears. "How could that possibly be?" He thought out loud.

McKellar analyzed the new information with Higgleton. They discussed the case, sharing opinions about the investigation, and information at hand. The one thing that nagged at them the most was the absence of a second male's DNA in that warehouse. How was it possible for Brooke to spend so much time in that warehouse, and not leave a single trace of his DNA? For which they still had no sample. They brainstormed on the subject for a while. Unable to find a logical explanation they decided to give it up for the moment. They left the diner, and each went back to their respective occupation promising each other to keep in touch with further developments.

Higgleton couldn't stop juggling that missing piece of the puzzle in his head. He decided to catch up with Geneva again. He didn't want to lose sight of her. He felt that her contact with Dale was still important in this case. Until they could locate Brooke Reese or Christa Makins, he had to keep close tabs on Geneva and Dale.

"So, am I cleared?" Geneva inquired the moment she saw Higgleton approach her, not missing a beat.

"Not quite yet. But don't worry, they don't know who and where you are."

"Then, why am I not cleared?"

"There are still too many unanswered questions, and I think you might be able to help answer them." Higgleton was serious in his response. So serious in fact that it was somewhat intimidating. Geneva let out a long full-hearted sigh.

"How can I possibly do that? I told you everything I know already." Geneva was exasperated and didn't bother trying to hide it.

"Do either Dale or Brooke work?" Higgleton attempted.

"Brooke works as a bartender at the Voo-Doo Lounge, but I don't know how that's going to help you." Geneva was a little insolent.

Higgleton ignored her attitude. He was used to people being difficult, especially when things weren't going as they hoped. Higgleton asked a few more questions. Geneva couldn't answer most of them. This case was starting to smell like Swiss cheese, there were too many holes in it.

Higgleton's next stop was the Voo-Doo Lounge, where, according to Geneva's information, Brooke worked. Higgleton learned from the owner that Brooke had taken a leave of absence. He had told his boss that his parents were sick, and he needed to go take care of them for a while. He would be back as soon as he could. Jim, the Lounge owner, was really disappointed to lose Brooke even if only for a short period of time, and assured Higgleton that he would welcome Brooke with open arms the moment he got back. He had never known a better bartender.

"Any idea where his parents live," Higgleton asked Jim.

"I never thought of asking," Jim looked stunned by his own ignorance. He slapped his forehead, "How could I not think of asking? Damn!"

"Happens all the time," Higgleton assured him. "Well, if you hear anything, please be sure to call me." He handed Jim his card, and walked out. Something didn't make sense why would Brooke go, but not Dale. Then he thought of the consequences if Dale were to miss school. He tried to convince himself that this was enough of an explanation, but deep down still felt something was amiss.

Higgleton decided to go back to watching Dale and Brooke's house. For a week, he watched while Dale was out, hoping to get a glimpse of Brooke. Nothing happened that whole week, not even a shadow in a window. The following week he followed Dale's every step hoping he would lead him to Brooke. Dale's routine was so that he went to school and back, then nothing outside an outing with Geneva. This house was too quiet to be normal. Higgleton still couldn't shake the feeling that he was missing something; something that he thought should be obvious.

Higgleton was going over the file again trying to find some of the missing pieces to the puzzle, when suddenly the name jumped right up at him. How could he have missed it before? It was right in front of him ever since he arrived to Thunder Bay. Yet, after spending a few weeks investigating, stalking, and raking his brain, he had missed the obvious. He looked through his notes to confirm his suspicion. Once satisfied with his conclusion he left his hotel room.

Dale and Brooke's last name was "Reese", just like Rebecca Reese. Why wouldn't she have mentioned them before? Maybe she didn't know of them. Higgleton decided to give her a call to find out. Their conversation was short. Ms. Reese didn't know them, nor of them. Higgleton knew this could not possibly be a coincidence.

He headed towards Andrew Street, walked up the steps where Geneva William lived. He rang the doorbell, and waited. It was late on a weeknight. A few minutes later a woman in her fifties, wearing curlers in her hair and an old scraggly housecoat, opened the door. The expression on her face said; she was not expecting any visitors, and wasn't too keen on receiving unexpected guest.

"I'm sorry to inconvenience you madam, but would Geneva William be in? I must speak with her." Higgleton showed compassion, but his voice stayed firm.

"Stay here, I'll get her. Who may I say is here?" Her voice was steel. The landlady closed the door, and turned the bolt on the lock. Higgleton heard it from outside where he waited. This lady was not going to let any strangers in. This comforted Higgleton. He knew that Geneva was safe in a home run by such a woman. Within minutes, Geneva was out the front door pulling her coat on.

"Let's walk," she said running down the steps. "We'll go have a coffee somewhere."

"Sure." They were both silent as they walked in the cold. The only sound they made was the crunching of the snow under their feet. Thunder Bay was still pretty cold in March. Snow didn't melt till mid to late spring this far north. They were both use to it. They both had spent their lives in this part of the world. Geneva led the way to the Café.

Coffee in hand, they sat in a booth in a far corner avoiding as many eavesdroppers as possible.

"What's up?" Geneva was the first to speak as she peeled the lid off her cup, and held her cold hands above the warm coffee.

"I have a very important question. You have to be one hundred percent sure about the answer you give me."

"Okay. What is it?"

"If I recall correctly you told me that Brooke lived with his twin brother. Is that correct?"

"Yeah! But what does that have to do with anything?"

"Would you happen to know if they are identical twins or fraternal twins?"

"Identical," Geneva didn't hesitate a second. "If they didn't dress and style their hair differently you wouldn't know which is which. But I still don't know what that has to do with anything." Geneva couldn't hide her confusion.

"DNA," Higgleton said with a smile on his face. He cocked his head sideways staring at Geneva, waiting for it to dawn on her. After a few minutes, he saw she didn't get it. He sat back in his seat, and added, "They share the same DNA. Identical twins have identical DNA patterns."

Even this bit of information flew right over her head. Geneva still didn't understand where Higgleton was going with this, but she was too tired to pursue the matter further. And he figured best to keep it this way.

They talked for a while, sipping their coffee. Geneva told Higgleton a few things she had noticed as odd. For one, she had never seen the two together. Never saw them home together, and sometimes she would notice identical mannerism in both.

"I don't know if any of this means anything, but I thought I'd share it with you." She said matter-of-factly, "More pieces that might or might not belong to the puzzle. But you really think the twins have something to do with the missing girl?" The question remained suspended in the air. Higgleton didn't want to divulge too much. Geneva would find out in time. Her friendship with them could work against him if she knew too much.

After walking Geneva back to her place, Higgleton walked around a little. Walking always helped him think. He tried to come up with a plan of action. He had to be careful how he approached the situation. He didn't want Christa going on the run again before he could reunite her with her aunt. He knew she deserved a good life, and that her aunt would provide it for her. Higgleton was a pretty good judge of character. He knew in his gut that Rebecca Reese was a good, honest person.

Higgleton needed more answers. He planned to search Brooke and Dale's house. He decided to check it out while Dale was in school one day. It was well into March now. The investigation had been going on for a while already. Higgleton wanted to close this case before the tracks got any colder. As soon as he was inside, he could not help notice how neat and clean the house was. That didn't seem normal for two young men residing alone. He knew there were no maids hired to clean the place. He had spent enough time watching; only one person ever came and went, Dale. Higgleton did a quick survey of the place. There was only one bedroom, and in it only one twin bed, odd for a place occupied by two. The furniture was scarce; the house only contained the necessities provided with a furnished agreement, which consisted of the bare necessities; bed, dresser, couch, fridge, stove, kitchen table and chairs, all very simple and distinctly old, purchased in the late fifties or early sixties. The furniture was still in very good condition. The place wasn't at all decorated other than the furniture. No personal touch had been added, except for a few magazines sitting on the end table next to the couch. Higgleton leafed through them. They were recent copies of Vogue, Oxygen (a woman's fitness magazine), and House & Home's 2005 Trends, another oddity for two males.

In the closet, very little clothing hung, and there was a noticeable division. One side had the plain, conservative clothing Higgleton had observed on Dale. The other half of the closet held trendier looking garments in bolder colours. In the dresser Higgleton found socks and underwear in the top drawer, pyjamas in the second, and the lower drawers contained sweaters. Everything was neatly folded, and in order of colour, lighter colours being on top. That too struck Higgleton as odd for two young males. How many guys sorted their clothes by colour? As he searched the bottom drawer his hand hit something hard under the left side pile of sweaters, a hidden diary. Higgleton pulled it out, and flipped through it. He noticed there was a time gap between each entry. The dates were usually a few days to a week or two apart, rarely two days in a row, and the latest entry was from the day before. This page was marked with an odd-looking card. It was slightly larger than a playing card, and much more colourful. A roman number marked the top of the card, XIII. Thirteen. Now, that added to the mystery of the card. Thirteen was also associated with many superstitions. The figure identifying the card was rather disturbing. A cloaked skeleton sat on a white horse, positioned on the ground around it were people laying lifelessly, and even nature around the figure looked pretty empty of life, almost as disturbing was the title below the figure, DEATH. He guessed this was a tarot card, but was clueless to its meaning. He would have to do a little research regarding this particular card. Higgleton's mind was racing. Could this have anything to do with the death of Christa Makins parents? Could their death not have been accidental? It was a scary, and unsettling thought. Higgleton decided to push it away until he knew more about this card.

From the irregularity with which entries were made, Higgleton concluded it was safe to take it for the night, and return it the next day.

Higgleton had spoken with the owner the day before using the pretext that he might want to invest in such a property. Unknowingly, the landlord had answered all of Higgleton's questions regarding Brooke and his brother. From his interview with the landlord Higgleton had found out that Dale had paid their rent for the whole year in cash. Dale had given the landlord cash in an envelope with a Sault Ste. Marie Mid-City Motel return address. The landlord hadn't asked too many questions assuming that the parents had sent the money, presuming that one of them probably worked at the Motel, and happy that he wouldn't have to chase rent every month. The Dale kid looked like a good, honest person, and he felt he was trust worthy. The landlord never met Brooke, but wasn't too concerned. He had no complaints about the boys, and hoped they would stay a while.

The bathroom revealed the more disturbing discoveries. He found women's hygiene products. The medicine cabinet contained cologne and masculine body spray and antiperspirant, but no razor, no shaving creams. There were also candles, sea salts, and other bath products. Something was very odd in this place. Nothing made sense. Higgleton had encountered many 'wackos' during his career both as an RCMP officer and as a P.I., but people's basic hygiene needs usually were pretty consistent with their gender, no matter what their sexual orientation, or preferences were.

Higgleton carefully left the house, and went back to his hotel. He wanted to read the diary, then get some sleep. His inspection of the house had raised new suspicions. Higgleton would be spending the whole night up watching for new clues. He wanted to be back before

Dale got back home. He had a feeling that the night might reveal a set of new clues. The more Higgleton discovered, the more he was surprised. In all his years, he had never encountered a case like this one. He was use to chasing criminals, and this was not a criminal, but someone who had planned a clever escape from her parents. It almost seemed like there were many runaways hiding in this small city hidden far north, and circled with forest and lakes. Had it not been for Christa Makins' DNA in that abandoned warehouse, Higgleton would never have found the trail to Thunder Bay.

He was sure that if Christa could have altered her DNA she probably would have changed that too, and really disappeared forever. This was one case Higgleton knew would have a happy ending. Christa could not possibly live this way the rest of her life. Complications would arise at one time or another. Eventually someone would discover her real identity. The worst was the stress she was putting on herself. Living in hiding could really take a toll on one's health; mental and physical.

THE DIARY

Settled in his hotel room, Higgleton sat in a reading chair with his feet up on the footstool, and diary in hand. The book was a six by eight inch burgundy leather bound with an imitation antique lock, and skeleton key. The key was in the lock when Higgleton found it, making his job a little easier. Not that a hairpin or paper clip couldn't have done the job. The pages also imitated weathered parchment with a decorative gold edge. Tucked in the edge of the diary, was a slim gold Cross pen held in by the clasp of the lock. These details told Higgleton that its owner treasured this diary. A lot of care had been put into choosing both the diary, and the pen. Higgleton got comfortable preparing for the long hours of reading ahead of him.

"Okay, Dale, Brooke, or whoever you are, what secrets do you hide," he questioned out loud. Higgleton had found the diary in the bedroom of Brooke and Dale's house. It was tucked in the bottom drawer of a dresser, under some clothing. Higgleton intended on returning the diary the very next day, which meant he had to read it all now. Luckily it was still early in the day. Higgleton opened the hard cover, and began reading.

Inside on a blank cover page the word 'Diary' was artistically handwritten with black ink. The letters were decorated with swirls, and the ends stretched into one another. Under the word 'Diary', also handwritten, were the initials 'C.M.', and under these was the following; 'From June 19, 2004 to' and a blank space. Those were also done up with swirls, and the works. These initials were the first clue confirming Higgleton's suspicions in Dale and Brooke's involvement with Christa Makins. He had to find out exactly what that involvement entailed. He turned the cover page, and began to read. The handwriting was a mixture: the author printed the capital letters, and followed with cursive small letters. From the penmanship Higgleton could tell that a female had most likely written this diary. Higgleton hoped the diary would give him the answer to Christa's whereabouts. He began to read;

Saturday June 19, 2004

Dear First Diary,

This is my very first diary, and hopefully not my last. In my old life, I could never have kept a diary. I did not have any privacy, not even a bed or a dresser of my own, hell, not even a drawer. My clothes were shoved in a corner, and good luck making out the clean from the dirty. This is a new beginning for me, and I am extremely excited.

Two days ago I finally took the big leap, and ran away. I just couldn't take it anymore. My birthday is coming up in the fall, and I couldn't bear the thought of what was coming. My imbecile parents always told me that the day I turned eighteen they expected me to support THEM. The way they put it, 'I was to return the favour'. Like hell I would ever support two drunks that never gave me much of a life to begin with. There was no favour to return. I had no childhood, and they worked me like a slave. Anyway, here is how it went;

It happened all so fast. I was arguing with my mother again, and something in me just snapped. Before things could get physical I ran out yelling, and never turned back. My mother and father are so out of shape, and always drunk that I knew they would never be able to follow. I always knew that someday I would run away. I was somewhat prepared.

I ran through the woods and just kept running until I reached my secret cave. I found this cave a few years ago during one of my many hiking trips. That was when the idea first came to me. Anyway… Everything I had prepared for this eventual day was waiting for me. I waited there

*until morning. The next day I drove into the sunrise to my
new life. I was so excited and, for the first time in my life, I
felt free. The air smelled purer, fresher. Even the sun seemed
to shine brighter, and I felt lighter. A huge weight had been
lifted from my shoulder,s or should I say two huge weights of
about three hundred pounds each. Anyway!*

*I rented a cute little house here, in Thunder Bay. I paid
the whole years' rent in cash. This way I don't have to worry
about it. I convinced the landlord that this was my parents'
idea. Little does he know that my parents could never gather
that much money in a whole lifetime even if their lives
depended on it. Thank God, they had no idea I had so much
money. They would have wasted it on more booze. I wonder
if they realize that I'm never coming back. I'm sure they don't
miss me. You can't miss someone you don't love or care about
to begin with. Maybe they haven't even noticed I'm gone yet.
They're always so drunk they have no clue what's going on
around them.*

*Well, that's it for today. Monday I have to get my
registration at Lakehead settled. I'll keep you up to speed.
My first diary, this is so much fun. I love living alone.*

Saturday June 26, 2004

*All is going according to plan. I was a little nervous
about getting into Lakehead, but it was easier than I
expected. I made up a story about having lost my acceptance
papers, and that surely they must have me on file. After a
few hours of pleading, they finally let me take the required
tests. I aced them. From research I had done at the library,
I knew there was a huge lack of students in Geoarchaeology.
I had studied everything I could find that was required to
get into this program. Choosing this field made it easier to
convince them of my file being lost in the system. I still can't
believe that I am registered in school, and this for the very
first time in my life. I'm sure not too many kids start school
directly in University. If my parents could see me now they*

would never believe it, especially my father who thinks girls can't amount to much. In your face dad! Losers! Both of them. God I'm so glad I got away from them. They definitely will never find me now.

Well, time for bed. I have another big day tomorrow. I have to find a job. I certainly don't want to use up all my savings. I've already put a dent in them with rent and tuition.

Monday June 28, 2004

Last night I discovered what the fuss of having a bath was all about. For the first time in my life I took a bath. I had read about it in a magazine and bought some sea salts and bath oils, and decided to find out firsthand what they were talking about. I had no idea that sitting in a tub of water could feel so good. I must have spent an hour in the bath. My hands and feet were wrinkled like prunes when I finally dragged myself out. I think I'll have one again tonight.

Before I forget, this morning I woke from a nightmare, when I woke up I was curled up in the corner of my bedroom bundled in my bedding. I saw myself back at my parents' house. I could smell the filthy stale air of their house. My heart felt like it was being squeezed, it hurt. I felt myself panic. I think I even screamed out loud. I'm not quite sure. I actually prefer to forget, but then I woke up for real, and realized it was only a nightmare. That I was here in my own clean home. It was such a relief to find that I wasn't anywhere near Echo Bay, but I was still shaking from the shock of it all. God, I never want to go back. I wonder if they're looking for me. Well, I'm not taking any chances. I am living incognito, and it's been working out pretty well.

Tuesday June 29, 2004

I found a great job at the Voo-Doo Lounge as a bartender. Dealing with drunken parents has paid off for the first time in my life. The owner decided to try me out immediately, and gave me the job before the evening ended. He was hesitant at first, but I finally got him to try me out without pay for one evening. Before the night was over, he dragged me into his office, and we discussed the details. I convinced him to pay me cash like I had done at the Motel in the Sault. I don't want to leave too many trails around. I'm still afraid of being found. I just couldn't live through another day around them, my parents that is. They are such a lost cause.

Friday July 2, 2004

I think I've really impressed the boss last night. The place was packed for the first of July celebration. I had the crowd eating in the palm of my hand. People are so predictable, especially when they drink.

The boss was so happy with my performance that he gave me a $50 bonus. That job is great! I get paid at the end of my shift every night, no waiting for my money. And I get to keep all my tips. That's where all the money is. Last night was quite a profitable evening. I raked in over $500 just in tips. Wow!

Now, I think I'll sleep all day. I'm so tired, and I work again tonight. I'm trying to work almost every night during the summer so that I can afford to work only part time when school starts.

Saturday July 3rd, 2004

Last night was another crazy night at the Lounge, but it paid really well. I never thought money could be made so easily, and quickly. It was a long night, and now I'm really tired. I think it's going to take me a few days to recuperate. Well, this is a short entry, but I don't have the energy to stay awake a minute longer.

Wednesday July 14th, 2004

I discovered an awesome gadget yesterday. It's called an iPod. It seems like everyone my age has one. Although I don't like to spend too much money I decided to treat myself to this great gadget. It works great with the Mac computer I also got for school. I got a great deal by buying both at the same time. It was hard to decide what kind of computer to buy. There is so much available, and I didn't know much about them. I shopped around until I found one I was comfortable with. I like all the funky graphics you can do with a Mac. Which is one of the reasons I chose it, also the salesperson was very insightful. He explained everything, and was very patient. He didn't make me feel like a fool like some of the other ones. I am discovering a love of music. I never realized how much is out there, all the different styles, and artists. Wow! I don't have any favourites yet, but I know that will soon change. I'm still discovering.

I wanted to get my computer ahead of time so I can get the hang of it before classes start. I'm glad I did. There is so much to learn. The computer was easier than I expected to set up. It's really user friendly. I think I'm going to have a lot of fun with this. I feel like a little kid getting a Christmas gift, not that I would know how that feels, but I imagine it's something like this.

This world is so different than the one I knew living with my parents. I have so much to learn, but I am trying not to attract too much attention to myself, which is sometimes hard when something new baffles me.

I'm back to work tonight. I get Sunday, Monday and Tuesday off.

Tuesday August 24th, 2004

I start class in a little over two weeks. I already have everything I need. I'm a little nervous about starting University. I've never been in a classroom before, so I don't really know how it works. I'll just have to follow the others, and see how it goes. It's kind of hard trying to look normal when everything is so new to me, but I'm slowly getting the hang of things. Sometimes I feel like I've traveled through time. There is such a contrast between my life in Echo Bay that seemed like something from the 19th century, and my life here, now.

Thursday September 2, 2004

I was out for a walk today, and discovered an area that seems completely abandoned, a part no one seems to talk about. It actually seems to be a taboo subject amongst the residents. I noticed this during conversations with customers at work. Every time I asked about it they quickly changed the subject. After my walk I went to work. I casually tried to inquire about it, but everyone just shied away from the subject. Tomorrow I think I'll see if I can find out anything about it at the library, or on the internet.

Well, time to sleep.

Thursday September 9th, 2004

Today was my first day of school. It's going to be harder than I expected. The classes are huge, and the teachers talk fast. I noticed some students had little devices that record the teachers' speeches. I think I should look into getting one. I think my iPod might have that kind of a feature. I'll have to check the manual. Well I have a lot to do before I go to work tonight, and tomorrow is another big day, and night.

I almost forgot. Some girl came to talk to me today, and gave me her number. This could get really awkward. I have to try to keep her away. Being invisible is going to be harder than I thought.

Friday September 10th, 2004

Remember that girl from yesterday, well I found out this morning that she lives across the street from me, how conveniently annoying. Now it's going to be even harder to avoid her. Just what I needed!

I ended up having to walk to school with her this morning then the rest of the day hiding from her. Can't I just have a quiet life ALONE? I don't have time for this shit!

Saturday September 18th, 2004

I got through another week. I'm so tired, but I think I'm starting to get the hang of it although I have to work really hard at it.

This girl I mentioned last week will not leave me alone. I'm not sure how to deal with it. She's really friendly, and seems to mean well. I'm just afraid of the awkwardness that can result with letting someone get close, especially a girl.

I work again tonight. Since school started I dropped Wednesday nights at the Lounge, but Thursdays and Fridays are pretty long with school during the day, and the Lounge at night. I wish I could sleep for a whole week. I'm so tired.

Thursday September 30ᵗʰ, 2004

School started less than a month ago, and I already wonder how I'm going to make it through the whole year. I've been trying a few different routines. It's hard to get by with only three or four hours of sleep between two twenty-hour days. Friday has to be the hardest day of the week, when the weekend comes all I want to do is sleep all day. I hope I adjust sometime soon, or I'll have to find a different way of bringing in money. This job is the only one I can think of that will bring this much money in, legally. And I don't do illegal.

The classes are good. It's so easy to go around unnoticed except from this one girl, Geneva. For some reason she seems to always seek me out, I can't seem to get her away from me. I've managed to hide a few times, but most days she finds me. She's also in my math class which makes it harder to avoid her. I tried cutting conversations short, but that doesn't seem to discourage her. She keeps suggesting we do stuff together, and I always blow her off. I'm afraid of starting a friendship, and have it turn into an awkward situation. It is kind of risky. I hope this girl gets the drift soon. I'm running out of ideas.

That's it for now. I need to get some sleep.

Tuesday October 5ᵗʰ, 2004

Today something weird happened. As usual Geneva came up to me. Today she suggested we do something together this coming Saturday. I blew her off, as usual, saying I had to study to which she offered her help. I lied, and said my parents didn't allow anyone in the house. What would my parents care, they don't even know where I am. They probably don't even miss me either, if they actually even remember who I am. She doesn't need to know that. Well, that's beside the point. I think I really hurt Geneva's feelings today. But back to the weird part, I actually felt bad about it. For almost a month I have been trying to get this girl away from me, and once I succeeded, I felt bad, and started seeking her out, but I couldn't find her anywhere. Tomorrow morning I'll make sure to catch her on the way to campus. I want to apologize for my rudeness. Maybe I should try a different approach. I'll explain to her that I'm not looking for friends. I'm too busy anyway, and maybe by telling her the truth she'll understand, and leave me alone, then I won't have to feel bad about being rude, or mean.

Sometimes, I feel like I'm part of a movie with different roles to play. I wake up being one person, then walk out as another, and at the end the day being yet a different person. It's kind of freaky that I can pull off such a performance. I never imagined I could do it so easily, and it doesn't look like anyone suspects anything either. Maybe I could become an actress. Well, Hollywood's a long way from here so I'll stick to Geoarchaeology for now. And my father didn't think girls could do much. Joke's on him.

Wednesday October 6th, 2004

Geneva was nowhere in sight today. I think I really pissed her off.

Friday October 8th, 2004

Geneva wasn't at school again today. After school I went to her house, and inquired about her. It seems that she has been sick. Now I know it wasn't me, but I still can't stop feeling bad about it.

Today is another one of those tough Friday's, but I found a new trick to help me get through my day and my night. I nap for a couple of hours after school, which makes such a difference. I think I'll make it to the end of the year after all. It's amazing what a nap can do.

Monday October 11ᵗʰ, 2004

Geneva's back. She came, and got me this morning. We walked together to campus. She is actually a pretty nice girl. I decided today to give this friendship thing a shot. I just hope it doesn't get mistaken for something else. I really would not know how to deal with such a misinterpretation. Well, anyhow, we are going to do some sightseeing on Saturday. I am actually looking forward to it, but at the same time I am kind of nervous. I have never had friends. I was too shy, and there were rarely any kids around when I was growing up. It's amazing how shyness dissipates when you are incognito.

I better get back to studying. I'll keep you posted on how it goes Saturday.

Sunday October 17ᵗʰ, 2004

Yesterday, Geneva and I went sightseeing. She had planned everything out. It was a full and fun day.

I got back just in time to get ready for work. She doesn't know about my job. I try to keep her away from that part of my life. I never thought that having a friend could be so pleasant. Some days I wish I could tell her everything, but the one thing I learned from my parents is that NO ONE can be trusted. Everyone has to fend for themselves, and sometimes that means having to keep secrets.

Monday November 22, 2004

Yesterday, Geneva came while Brooke was at the house.
It gave me a chance to see a different side of her. I couldn't
have planned it any better if I tried.

She hit it off pretty well with Brooke. I think his looks
might have helped. She looks at him differently than she
looks at Dale. There was a twinkle in her eye I had never
seen before. Brooke showed her his secret hideaway, and
made plans to see her again this coming Wednesday, one of
his nights off.

Geneva is so easy to get along with that it's getting harder
not to tell her about the three of us, but I just can't take the
risk.

Wednesday December 15, 2004

I can't believe what just happened. I was just talking
with Geneva quietly in the park when suddenly she tried to
kiss me. Freaked me right out. How could she do that? Girls
are not supposed to put the move on guys, are they? Or is
that only in the movies? Now I don't know how to deal with
this. I can never let her see Brooke again. She'll ruin it for
all of us. God, I wish I could tell her everything just to avoid
further issues. But if she ever found out I don't think she
would ever speak to either of us again.

When I see her again tomorrow, I'll just have to pretend
nothing ever happened.

Higgleton continued reading each page. He had already found
much of the information he had been looking for. He had a pretty good
idea where to find Christa. Reviewing all the information encountered
since his arrival to Thunder Bay, Higgleton couldn't help thinking
about the old saying; 'We often can't see what is right in front of us'.

Christa had really planned her escape well. Had it not been for the
dead body found in the abandoned warehouse they would never have
found her. The presence of her DNA was the only thing that gave her

away. She was a smart girl, and had constructed her plan meticulously, at least for the short term. Higgleton continued reading. He still had quite a few pages still to read.

Tuesday December 14, 2004

> *Geneva and I will be celebrating Christmas together. I really don't know what to expect, but she seems to know what to do, and what we need. I'll just follow her lead...*

Monday December 27, 2004

> *This year was my first time celebrating Christmas. Although it was only Geneva and I, it was great. We had a beautiful home cooked meal. Geneva is a great cook. After dinner we watched movies till four o'clock in the morning. Then Geneva went home and I slept all day.*
> *I now have a whole new perspective on Christmas, thanks to Geneva. She really is a great friend.*

Higgleton couldn't help wonder how long Christa would have kept this charade if she wasn't discovered. What kind of life would she have lived in this hidden identity? He wondered if she had thought that far. Higgleton's mind wandered. Thinking about what makes people choose drastic changes. He had seen a lot of unimaginable characters in his career, and heard many horror stories in the courtroom. One's childhood really shapes their future. Not everyone has what it takes to be a good parent, and money has nothing to do with it. We need permits for just about everything except parenting, yet the damage that some parents do is horrifying, and can sometimes ruin several lives. This was always a sore point for Higgleton. He cherished children, and felt tightness to his heart every time he came across a case where children had been mistreated, or abused. Only cowards could do such things. He continued reading;

Sunday January 2nd, 2005

    Geneva and I brought the New Year in together. We had a nice dinner at my place and toasted with bubbly wine at midnight. We played cards, and laughed all night.

    After Geneva went home I sat down, and started writing down my new year resolutions. Here they are;

    1-Have fun, find new adventures to try.
    2-Keep up the good schoolwork and plan my career.
    3-Be a good friend to Geneva. Always be there for her.

    Well, that's all that I came up with. I don't need to lose weight, like all these silly magazines seem to suggest. I know there's more to life than money, but I still want to be rich someday. So I thought I should concentrate on what makes me happy; Geneva, school and laughter.

Tuesday January 18, 2005

    Today a body was found in the warehouse I used as a sanctuary away from everyday life. Now, I don't know if I will ever be able to go back. The news said the victim was a female loafer whom they suspected died of natural causes, but an investigation is still being performed to confirm. With police crawling all over the place I won't be able to go there for a while at least. I hope the cats don't die of hunger. I'm going to miss them so much. I hadn't realized that anyone else went in that warehouse when I wasn't there. I wish I had made a door right at the beginning, and this could have been avoided.

    I wonder how thorough an investigation they intend on doing. Could they possibly link my presence in that warehouse? I hope not. That could have some serious consequences for me. I have to admit, I'm a little worried. I'll have to keep my eyes and ears open.

    I feel like I'm part of a bad horror movie.

Tuesday February 15, 2005

    I just spent the worst twenty-four hours of my life, not counting the years I lived with my parents. I thought the coast was clear, and decided to go check on the cats yesterday. Guess what? I was arrested. Can you believe that? I walked into the warehouse, and found myself surrounded by cops. I was so surprised, and scared. Then they kept me at the station all night, questioning me about myself. That I have to admit was a little ironic, but I think I gave them a pretty good performance. I must have since I'm back here writing in my diary. Thank God they didn't body search me, or take a DNA sample.

    When I got home I took a long shower I felt so dirty, then I relaxed in a nice, long, hot bath, but now I can't sleep. My mind is racing around the events of the night. I have to think of how to make this issue go away. I just can't let them find me. I just can't. I never want to go back to Echo Bay.

    That's it for now. I have some thinking to do.

Wednesday February 16, 2005

    After I was arrested, I decided to quit my job at the Lounge. This is really making things rather complicated. That stupid body they found in the warehouse has been giving me a lot grief. I do feel sorry for that poor woman, but her body has practically brought the police straight to my doorstep. If they find me, it's over. No more Brooke, no more Dale, and hell all over again. I can't bear the thought.

It took Higgleton a few hours to get through the whole diary. Its content confirmed most of his suspicions, it even shed some light on other areas. Once finished he turned the closed diary around in his hands, observing its details. It had the look of an old fashion book. The cover was thick and sturdy. Looking more closely he noticed that the front cover was thicker than the back. From the spine, Higgleton noticed an opening. He got up to get tweezers from his toiletries, and came back to sit in the reading chair. Patiently he pulled out a folded sheet of paper hidden in the diary's front cover. Higgleton slowly unfolded the paper. It was a birth certificate. The name on the certificate was Christa Dale Makins. Higgleton read further mother's name; Sara Brooke Reese, and father; Hank Errol Makins. Higgleton walked out of his room, and went to the front desk to make a copy. He had to keep a copy for when came time to explain his theory to Frank. No one would want to believe it.

The next day he would put the diary back while Dale was in school. Hopefully, Dale would never notice it was missing. Now, he had to call Jack, and set up the next move.

March 28, 2005, before making his way to the police station Higgleton decided to stop at the library on Red River Road just off Algoma Street. It was only a few minutes away from the Thunder Bay Police Station. He had to know the meaning of that tarot card from Christa Makins diary. The birth certificate had confirmed the ownership of the diary, and had given Higgleton the missing pieces to the puzzle. Dale, Brooke, and Christa, all were linked. Only one birth certificate had all the names, and clues he had needed to solve it all.

As soon as Higgleton walked into the library the smell of old books hit him like a wall. He quickly found a computer station and typed the word 'Tarot' as the key word for his search. Immediately the computer spit all the results of available books on the subject. He noted the most common three first digits of the entire selection, and made his way through isles loaded with shelves filled with books of all sizes, and colours.

Higgleton grabbed four books on the subject, and brought them to a nearby table. He sat down, opened the first book, and scanned the index. Almost immediately he found the title of the card he wanted to know more about. He flipped to the referred page, and began to read, then repeated this procedure a second, a third, and a fourth time. Although each book had its own version of the meaning of the 'Death' card the basics remained the same. This card represented the end of something in order to allow the beginning of something else. It could be a project, a relationship, a life style, but it was an end towards a new beginning, usually nothing to do with a physical death. Higgleton was somewhat relieved to read this. He had a hard time imagining Christa Makins premeditating her parents' death, but stranger things had happened. He had seen too many of them first hand. Deep down he had high hopes for this girl. He really wanted her to have the break she deserved which was why he so desperately wanted to find her, and soon, because the sooner she was united with her aunt, the sooner she could put the past behind, and start her new life. A real one this time.

Higgleton made a copy of the most intelligible description of this card before walking out of the library. He knew McKellar might have a good laugh at him, but he didn't care. Higgleton always liked to have all the physical support he could get for any theory he brought to the table. Surprisingly, many police personnel had not yet realized how twisted this world really is. Reality was often far more twisted than fiction.

COMPLETING THE PUZZLE

April 3rd 2005, a police car parked in front of the Reese house on Andrew Street.

It was a gloomy Sunday morning when Dale heard the chime from the doorbell. He was at the kitchen table having breakfast. He quickly got up, and opened the door expecting to see Geneva. Instead Dale saw two policemen on his doorstep. Of course they were wearing their uniform, and all the radios and gadgets they use on their job. Both were pretty tall around the six-feet, but one was a couple of inches taller than the other. That kind of height made them seem rather impressive. It didn't make you want to mess with them. They both had dark hair, but one wore a crew cut while the other had his hair in a short stylish spike. Dale couldn't help notice how handsome and young they were, but he still had to resist the urge of slamming the door shut, and running to hide. Instead, he concentrated very hard on acting normal.

"Good morning, how may I help you?" Dale answered trying to look normal, but feeling very nervous. He had a pit in the bottom of his stomach because he felt this had something to do with Brooke.

"Excuse us for disturbing you, but does Brooke Reese live here? We would like to speak with him." They stood at the door looking inside searching for their suspect.

"Yes, he does, but he isn't in right now. Is there a message?" Dale was trying hard to keep his calm. His body was starting the feel weak. He could feel sweat breaking. He kept his hands in his pocket to hide the fact that they were shaking.

"Would you have any idea where we could find him?" The officer with the stylish spikes did all the talking. He smiled as he asked Dale these questions.

Dale thought to himself, 'He's smiling to trick me into relaxing'.

"No, sir, I'm sorry I have no idea where Brooke is. He never tells me of his whereabouts."

"Are you Dale Reese?" said the other police officer.

"Yes, I am." Dale said in return, keeping a straight face.

"Is Brooke Reese your identical twin?"

"Yes, he is." He was wondering where these cops were going with this line of questioning.

"Could you, please, come to the station with us?"

"Do I have to?" Dale got really nervous when the cop asked him to go with them. So many things were flashing through his head. How could this possibly be happening? How could he be in trouble when all he did was go to school, come home, study, and sleep?

"Dale, we just need to verify some information with you. You don't have to worry about a thing." Red flags kept popping in his head. He really didn't want to go with them to the station, but Dale couldn't find any valid excuse not to go.

He couldn't help wondering how this all came about. He knew this was the end of Brooke and him. He should have known it would come to this one day.

At the police station, they put Dale in a room. He never saw the two young officers again. They made him wait for a while then different officers came to ask a few questions. They were older, and more experienced he assumed. After a long period of questioning the cops asked for a DNA sample. Dale tried to protest as much as he possibly could, but after arguing a while he had no valid approach. They took a swab of his saliva, and disappeared through the door. Dale was alone in the room for a long while this time, he couldn't tell how long it had been. There was no clock in this room. The walls were completely bare. The room was empty with the exception of two folding chairs, a folding table, and him. He was starting to feel like he was part of the furniture. Dale felt as grey as their painted metal frames.

Suddenly, calmness came over him, a sense of peace. He knew that the moment they came back it would be over. He simply had to accept that fact. They would know his true identity, and Brooke and Dale would no longer exist. What he didn't know was where they would send him. His parents? Jail? A mental institute? That was the remaining mystery. He could deal with the latter two, but not the first. He would rather die than go back to his horrible parents. He sat there, and waited. It was probably the longest he had to wait in his life. Time goes by so slowly when your entire life is at stake.

Higgleton's phone rang later that Sunday. Jack McKellar updated Higgleton on the results of the Reese DNA test. The whole department was stumped.

"How did you know?" Jack said to Higgleton.

"It was right in front of us the whole time," answered Higgleton.

"What do you mean," asked Jack. Higgleton then went into great detail about the last name of Rebecca and the boys, then the resemblance of the sketch of Christa and the boys.

"Unless she was also their twin no one could have so much resemblance. I have a complete file for you including a copy of her birth certificate which also fills many of the holes," explained Higgleton. "Can I get her aunt to come get her?"

After hanging up with Jack McKellar, Higgleton called Rebecca Reese. The familiar female voice answered. Without even introducing himself Higgleton simply blurted out;

"We found her."

"Are you sure?" Rebecca Reese was excited yet fearful of getting her hopes up too high, and had to ask the following; "Alive?"

"Yes, alive and kicking. Now get yourself on a plane. I'll pick you up at the airport," Higgleton ordered.

"You're really that sure?" Rebecca's voice was shaky. She had to sit. The overwhelming feeling of joy was more powerful than she would have ever imagined. Hearing the confidence in Higgleton's confirmation made the world spin around her at a thousand miles an hour. So many emotions ran through her at once.

"I'll call you back with my flight number." They both disconnected, and Rebecca Reese ran to her computer to book her flight. She was a pro at making travel arrangements. She always made her own flight and hotel arrangements. The first few years when she had started her business she had practically lived out of a suitcase. She was never home more than a week at a time. Her travels had settled down a little, but she still had to travel at least a week every couple of months. Now, she intended on showing Christa the world.

Rebecca just threw some clothes in an overnight bag which already contained a spare set of toiletries. With all that travel, it was a necessity to have doubles of everything she used daily in her travel bag. This way she never forgot anything.

On her way to the airport she called Higgleton with the specifics.

Finally, what felt like hours later at the police station, the door opened again, and a woman walked into the interrogation room closing the door behind her. She looked very sophisticated. She wore quality clothes; black slacks with a light blue silk blouse under a black suit jacket. Everything fell perfectly in line with her body. Dale wondered if her clothes weren't tailor made. Even her make-up was perfect, and her hair was professionally styled. A beautiful scent followed her into the room. He could tell she was not with the police department. She looked too expensive.

"I don't need a lawyer. Besides, I have no money to afford one." He said as soon as she approached the table to sit in front of him.

"I'm not a lawyer, Christa," the woman said with a smile.

"Why are you calling me Christa?" Asked Dale, fear in his eyes.

"You can stop the act Christa the police know who you really are. The DNA results confirmed it." The woman said in a calm voice. "I have something very important to tell you about your parents, and about your future." Christa noticed the woman was shaking, and looked as nervous as she, herself felt. The woman's eyes transpired a mixture of feelings. Christa couldn't understand why. Who was this woman? Why would she care about her?

"Oh! No! I'm not going back there." Christa screamed, "If you send me there I will kill myself. I would rather die than go back to live with them." Before she finished saying this Christa stood up, and was pacing the room. She felt bewilderment beyond her control. The lady stood up, and cautiously approached her. She opened her arms, and Christa could see tears building in her eyes.

"No, no. You are not going back. I promise you that. You are coming with me," she said in a soft patient voice. Christa looked up at her. Her face was sincere. Her eyes were looking straight into Christa's. "I'm your family now," she said with a smile. Tears were rolling down her cheeks.

"I don't understand," Christa had not come within reach of her. She didn't like to be approached by strangers, and this lady was a stranger to her. The woman let her arms fall by her sides, and smiled, in a way that let Christa know she understood. Tears still rolling down the woman's cheeks.

"Come sit, I'll explain. Trust me, I only want what is best for you." Christa followed her back to the table. They sat facing each other. "My name is Rebecca Reese. I don't know if you ever heard my name before."

Christa simply shook her head.

"I'm your mothers' older sister." She closed her eyes for a short second then looked back into Christa's, "Your parents died in a house fire last June. Do you know anything about the fire?"

Christa's eyes went wide with surprise, and a lump formed in her throat. She had no idea what the woman was talking about. What fire? How? When? Her mouth kept opening and closing like a fish, but no sound came out. Rebecca Reese put a hand on Christa's arm.

"It's okay. Let it out, you can let the tears fall. I didn't think I would cry when my parents died, but I too was as shocked as you are now. Family ties are funny that way."

She was right, never had Christa expected to feel the sadness and pain of losing her parents. When she had left, she never wanted to see them again, but now that she knew that she could never see them again it was different. Now, Christa didn't have a choice in the matter. The door was closed forever.

"How did it happen?" She barely managed to speak. Her throat felt constricted, tears were rolling down her face, and her nose was adding to the falls. Rebecca told Christa about the fire, and her parents passing. She gave Christa a detailed account of the incident. Christa couldn't help feeling responsible for their death. Then it flashed in her head. She suddenly remembered hitting something as she ran out.

"Oh! My God! It's my fault. Oh! My God! I killed them. What's going to happen to me? Am I going to jail? What did I do?" Rebecca assured Christa that it was an accident, and that she shouldn't put any blame on herself, but Christa couldn't help feel like it was all her fault.

"I've been looking for you ever since I found out about the fire, and your parents death." She told Christa about Higgleton, and all the dead ends they had encountered until that body was found in the warehouse where Christa's DNA was discovered.

"I've dreamt of this day since you were a baby. I always thought of you as mine, but your mother pushed me away. I'm so sorry I wasn't there for you while you were growing up. You here, now, this is the answer to my long awaited prayers," Rebecca said.

Christa simply looked silently at her aunt. She didn't know what to say. This was a lot for her to take in all at once.

"I promise you will never lack anything again for the rest of your life. You will get the best education, and I want to show you the world. We will travel all over the globe." Rebecca felt she was getting ahead of herself. "If you're interested, that is. You don't have to do anything you don't want." Rebecca's eyes were glowed with pride and joy.

"This is… It's more than I could have ever hoped," Christa was having a difficult time speaking. She was overwhelmed with gratitude, and didn't know how to express it.

Before leaving the station, Christa inquired about the kittens and their mother. They assured her that the SPCA had been contacted, and homes would be found for them. Knowing this allowed her to leave a little more light hearted, although she would miss them.

That same night Christa and Rebecca flew first class to Chicago together after picking up Christa's few belongings from the house. It all felt like a dream. Christa was expecting to wake up any moment to find out that it was all just a fantasy.

While Rebecca Reese was getting acquainted with her niece Higgleton was meeting with Chris Carnell and Jack McKellar. Before his meeting, Jack went to Carnell's office.

"Chris! I have information on your case." Jack explained to Carnell his relation with Higgleton, and Higgleton's role in the Christa Makins case.

"I think you should come with me," he said to Carnell

McKellar and Carnell walked into the boardroom where Higgleton was already waiting. Higgleton introduced himself to Chris Carnell, and confirmed that Jack had explained his position. This was always the hard part, explaining all the reasons for breaking protocol, and ensuring that his friends' career would not suffer from his association. Usually, he was able to smooth things over pretty easily, but he never took it for granted. One day he would meet a hard nose cop that did not appreciate his interference. Not today. Today, Chris Carnell thanked him for his help and discretion in the matter, but suggested that Higgleton not make a habit of it.

"Don't worry. This was my last case; after things are tied up here my retirement begins."

"One more thing, where are you from," Carnell asked Higgleton before letting him go. "Higgleton is a rather unusual name for this part of the country."

"My great-great-grand father was English, but I was born in Homepayne." Higgleton didn't offer more. Everyone parted peacefully. Higgleton thanked McKellar for his support, and wished him the best.

EPILOGUE

"Wow!" My reaction was spontaneous as I walked into my aunt's place. I couldn't have stopped it if I tried. It was everything I had always dreamed about; ceiling to floor windows with a view of the lake, the most contemporary furniture I had ever laid eyes on. It was better than anything I had seen in all those magazines. With just one look around me I knew Aunt Rebecca and I had a lot in common.

She showed me to my room where I even had my own Ensuite. I couldn't believe I had my own room, my own bathroom. It had a separate bath and shower. The bathtub was bigger and deeper than any I had ever seen. I couldn't wait to have a soak in it. Surrounding the tub were salts, oils, and other things I would have to ask Aunty Rebecca about. The bedroom alone was almost bigger than the place I had rented in Thunder Bay, and the closet was as big as a small room. I had more space than I knew what to do with. I was truly amazed.

I felt too wired to sleep yet, and Aunty Rebecca had already wished me good night. After pacing the room admiring it's every detail, I enjoyed a long hot bath, and was finally able to get myself in bed, and sleep.

The next day I woke in my new home. Aunty Rebecca assured me lawyers would take care of tying all the loose ends with the Thunder Bay Police Department. That all I had to worry about was healing my broken spirit, and that she would be there for me every step of the way. She had been through it herself, and showed me how we can actually change our destiny if we actually believed in ourselves.

As we were finishing breakfast the doorbell rang. Aunty Rebecca went to answer. She came back holding a box bearing holes and that seem a little unstable in her arms.

"I have a surprise for you," she looked at me with smiles in her eyes. She held the box out for me to take it.

"For me?" I took the box slowly. I didn't know what to expect until I heard a meow coming from it. I immediately put the box down on the floor, and hurried to open it. Inside was Butler, one of the kittens I had found in the warehouse where I had built my little retreat. "How did you get him?" I couldn't finish my question, but Aunt Rebecca knew exactly what I was trying to say.

"I have my ways," was all she said about how she got Butler. "Your friend Geneva is keeping the mother and the other kitten. Her landlord gave her consent. How would you like it if we invited her here for the summer?"

"Are you serious?" I was overjoyed, but then I suddenly got nervous, "does she know?"

Aunt Rebecca told me about Higgleton, and the role he played in finding me. He had told her about Geneva. So after we had picked up my belongings, she sent him across the street to speak to Geneva. She knew how important friends are, and wanted to at least try to save this friendship.

Soon I would discover how resourceful this woman was. She was the most amazing woman I would ever meet. Every day I thank the Gods for bringing her into my life.

For the second time in my life, I felt that same feeling I had felt driving away from Echo Bay. Another weight was lifted. In my mind I buried Dale and Brooke. I no longer needed them. My therapist assured me that the scars would heal, and that eventually I would be proud to be Christa Reese. I had chosen to change my last name this was another step towards this new chapter in my life.

"Finish up your breakfast. We have a busy day ahead of us."

I looked at my aunt, and she saw the question in my eyes.

"We have to go shopping," she said with a smile. "You didn't think I was going to let you continue dressing like a boy." We both laughed, and continued discussing plans for that day as we finished our breakfast.

Aunt Rebecca is really easy to get along with. I could not have asked for a better home and mentor.

Geneva is still attending Lakehead, but we spend all our holidays together.

ACKOWLEDGEMENTS

First and foremost, I would like to thank Michael for believing in me, and encouraging me to pursue my dream. Thank you, Baby!

Secondly, I thank my family and friends that have taken the time to read my manuscript, discuss the story's strengths and weaknesses, and encouraged me to pursue publication.

I would also like to thank Paul Connell of the OPP for answering my questions about police ranks, procedures, and jurisdictions.

Last, but not least, I thank all of you who have read my novel, and I hope you will continue to read my stories. If you are a fan come visit me at www.nerolibooks.ca.

Printed in the United States
127328LV00001B/595-621/P